I0638035

Endgames

Octavius Bear

Meets

Sherlock Holmes

and the

Glamorous Ghost

Harry DeMaio

© Copyright 2024

Harry DeMaio

The right of Harry DeMaio to be identified as the author of this work has been asserted by him in accordance with the Copyright, Designs and Patents Act 1998.

All rights reserved. No reproduction, copy or transmission of this publication may be made without express prior written permission. No paragraph of this publication may be reproduced, copied or transmitted except with express prior written permission or in accordance with the provisions of the Copyright Act 1956 (as amended). Any person who commits any unauthorised act in relation to this publication may be liable to criminal prosecution and civil claims for damage.

All characters appearing in this work are fictitious. Any resemblance to real persons, living or dead, is purely coincidental. The opinions expressed herein are those of the author and not of MX Publishing.

Paperback ISBN 978-1-80424-520-0
ePub ISBN 978-1-80424-521-7
PDF ISBN 978-1-80424-522-4

Published by MX Publishing
335 Princess Park Manor, Royal Drive,
London, N11 3GX
www.mxpublishing.co.uk

Cover design by Brian Belanger

Dedicated to GTP

A Most Extraordinary Bear

And to the late Ms. Woof

An Extremely Sweet

and Loving Dog

Also by Harry DeMaio

The Octavius Bear Series – Books 1-20

1-The Open and Shut Case

2-The Case of the Spotted Band

3-The Case of Scotch

4-The Lower Case

5-The Curse of the Mummy's Case

6-The Attaché Case

7-The Suit Case

8-The Crank Case

9-The Basket Case

10-The Camera Case

11-The Wurst Case Scenario

12-The Nut Case

13-A Case of Déjà Vu

14-The Case of Cosmic Chaos

15-A Case for the Birds

16-The Cases Down Under

17-The Octavian Cases

18-The Bear Faced Liar

19-Bears at Sea

Special Note to the Reader

Endgames! The closing moves in chess. While there are Queens and Pawns in the pages, this book is not about the board game!

This is the last volume in the Glamorous Ghost and Octavius Bear cycles. The time has come to hit the Ctrl/End keys on Microsoft Word one last time and shut down the system. *(Not entirely true. The twentieth book in the Octavius Bear collection -The Case of the Polar Politician . and the fourth book of the Glamorous Ghost series have recently been published. Please give them a look! Thank you!)*

I've had a lot of fun with Lady Juliet Armstrong, Pookie, Sherlock Holmes, Doctor Watson, Mrs. Hudson and the Baroness' entourage of celestial celebrities as they chase around heaven and earth in pursuit of madmen, muggers and murderers. Oh yes, throw several thieves and kidnappers into the mix. I hope you've shared that enjoyment.

Octavius Bear, the Octavians and their cast of bad guy opponents have also found their share of eager readers for their earthbound and interplanetary hi-jinks. Now, for the first time, Holmes, the Celestials and Octavians meet and more adventures abound.

Thank you so much for spending your valuable time with my offbeat characters, tongue-in-cheek dialogue and absolutely 'thrilling' plot lines. I have acknowledged my supporters and enthusiasts elsewhere in this tome. I am most grateful to them all as I am to you.

To view the entire array of books and get a bit more background, please go to my website/blog –

www.tavighostbooks.com or look me up on

MXPublishing.com.

Now, on to this volume of madcap mysteries of mischief and mayhem. Whenever I am asked to sign one of my books, I add the following inscription – **"I hope you enjoy this."**

I truly do!

Harry DeMaio

Prologue

Another Sherlock Holmes Pastiche! We're back yet again with tongues firmly but respectfully in cheeks. Say 'Hello' once more to Sherlock Holmes, Consulting Detective Extraordinaire. Welcome back Lady Juliet Armstrong, Baroness Crestwell and the nine foot tall Kodiak, Octavius Bear with his wife, offspring and entourage, the Octavians.

(What's a pastiche, anyway? Let's see what Wikipedia has to say. *"A **pastiche** is a work of literature, visual art, theatre, music, or architecture that imitates the style or character of the work of one or more other artists. Unlike parody, pastiche pays homage to the work it imitates, rather than mocking it. The word pastiche is French and describes works that are either composed by several authors, or that incorporate stylistic elements of other artists' work."*)

Holmes, Watson and Mrs. Hudson need no further introduction. The original Conan Doyle canon, pastiches, stage and screen plays, TV series and a healthy supply of Holmes miscellania exceed a thousand items and who knows how many followers.

Less well known but accumulating a rapidly increasing number of fans, Lady Juliet Armstrong Baroness Crestwell is front and center. A former sensation of the London musical stage; a feisty member of the British nobility by marriage but recently, a most definitely ***deceased*** arrival at the Elysian Fields. The obstreperous noblewoman was not content to don her halo and bland heavenly garb and join the other celestial denizens in eternal bliss. She had been shot and wanted to find the blighter who did it and bring him/her to justice before going to her eternal reward. Who else to solve the mystery than

1

Sherlock Holmes and Doctor Watson? Clad in her scarlet Parisian evening gown and wearing a chic corona fashionably tilted on her head, she persuaded the powers that be in Heaven to allow her to return to Earth and seek out Sherlock Holmes' assistance. Holmes, no believer in ghosts, reluctantly acknowledged the noblewoman's otherworldly existence and agreed to cooperate with her in what has evolved into a series of rollicking semi-supernatural adventures. Watson and Mrs. Hudson joined in.

Now, it's inevitable. Separated by over a century in time and millions of light years in distance, Octavius Bear, his wife Bearoness Belinda, their twin son and daughter and their cohort, the Octavians, are about to embark on a joint mission with Holmes and Lady Juliet. Interplanetary adventures! In twenty volumes, Octavius and his associates have taken on all manner of crime and criminal in a wide variety of locales on what we call Earth Alpha. Highly intelligent and incredibly wealthy, they represent the ultimate in the sentient animals who survived the long ago demise of Homo Sapiens due to a devastating solar storm. Now they join the immortal Baroness Juliet and the very mortal Sherlock Holmes in Endgames.

Let's not forget another ghostly and no less glamorous character who aids and abets throughout. Pookie, Juliet's ethereal dog, a very clever and highly opinionated Bichon Frisé. She predeceased her Baronial mistress but waited for her at the Rainbow Bridge outside Paradise. She barks, whines and wags her way into the proceedings at every turn but doesn't talk. She's an accomplished aerobatic flier and winner of Top Gun status with the True Angel's Flight Demonstration Team. She performs with the Lipizzaner Stallions and Pegasus and plays multi-dimensional fetch in the Meadows with her canine companions. Unruly as her owner, she is always instrumental in keeping the action going.

Pookie will come in contact with Madame Giselle Woof. Another Bichon in another world. Fully sentient and an expert in Tarot Cartomancy, she's a very important Octavian.

In Books Two through Four, the Baroness and her dog continued their excursions from Paradise back to Earth Beta with Holmes and the good Doctor. She and Pookie flitted to locations around the world but always returned to their heavenly mansion under the careful scrutiny of Director Raymond and the Committee. Becoming aware of the two winsome wraiths, Mrs. Hudson also linked up with the merry band.

Now, of course, Baroness Juliet will meet Bearoness Belinda. "Les Elegantes." Multiverse female nobility on crime fighting missions.

Many other characters also pass through these pages. All the Octavians and their associates are present and accounted for. Later entries including Juliet's family and the wonderful Lipizzaner stallions are on hand. The madcap mystical mischief and mayhem carries on under Director Raymond's angelic guardianship and the Heavenly Committee's scrutiny. Old and new characters, situations and adventures abound. Here are the Virgin Mary and St. Joseph. To say nothing of Queen Victoria, Prince Albert, Empress Sisi, King Edward VII, Queen Alexandra, Chief Inspector Lestrade, Confucius, Leonardo DaVinci, George Frideric Handel, Saints Francis and Cecilia. So much for the notables. There are scores of ordinary folks filling our pages. And on the wise but non-verbal side, we have Pookie, Pegasus, Unicorn and more of the Lipizzaner Stallions. Join us for more fantasy and lighthearted fun where highly talented animals, ghosts, angels, saints nobles and ordinary humans get together in multiple worlds over a century apart!

Several chapters in this book are adapted from my short story *Doctor Bear, I Presume!* published by Belanger Books in 2019 in the Anthology *Sherlock Holmes Adventures in the Realm of Steampunk Volume Two.*

Chapter One

"Now, there is only one true God in three persons, Creator of Heaven and Earths."

"Earths? Plural?"

"Yes, Baroness, throughout the Multiverse, in an incredible number of galaxies, there are an immense number of exoplanets circling a huge number of individual or sometimes multiple stars. Some are barren and lifeless, at least for the moment. They may be a potential inventory for future worlds. But some support life forms now, not necessarily as you know them. The Creator has an infinite number of designs at His disposal and an infinite number of galaxies in which to express them. I and my fellow cosmologists and astronomers have had to seriously revise our thinking upon our entry into Paradise and being faced with celestial realities."

This lesson in Cosmology by Nicolaus Copernicus had been commissioned by Mary, the Queen of Heaven through Director Raymond. Lady Juliet Armstrong, Baroness Crestwell was seated in a comfortable reclining armchair in a lecture hall equipped with multidimensional projections and sound. State of the art Virtual Reality holographic technology without benefit of headsets provided vivid images and action as they swooped from world to world. The Baroness was breathless from the experience. Pookie, confused, had hidden under the chair.

She was accompanied by several angels and other deceased mortals like herself. Her Imperial Majesty Elisabeth (Sisi), former Empress of Austro Hungary was seated next to her. Mr. Sherman, caretaker of the Meadows, home of deceased but unaccompanied animals, was in attendance. So were her great friends Galileo, DaVinci and Confucius. St. Catherine of Alexandria, patroness of philosophers was seated pensively in the back of the room. She would have to reconsider some of her basic assumptions. St. Ursula, the patron saint of school girls was up front, earnestly taking copious notes. There were several other attendees with whom Juliet was unacquainted. The angels in luminescent garb were carefully watching the attendees and the presentation.

Pookie had finished off her snack of several Heavenly Chewies and curled up for a snooze at Lady Juliet's feet.

Juliet turned to Director Raymond, flashing her enigmatic smile. "Angelic Sir. I and my friends here appreciate the tutorial you and the Queen have arranged and I am most eager to learn more about the Multiverse and its alternate worlds. I, like most of my contemporaries always believed we were alone in the Cosmos. I suspect Signori DaVinci and Galileo knew otherwise and perhaps Master Kong *(Confucius)* as well. Thank you! But I am confused as to why we are having this session."

"You are about to be asked to go on a mission, milady. You and several of your companions. You may refuse, of course, but knowing your inquisitive and venturous nature, I doubt you will pass it up."

"But why are we talking about other planets?"

"Because that's where the Queen of Heaven would like you to go. First you will meet the denizens of a very different but in many ways very similar world. They call it Earth Alpha. They are anthropomorphic animals, very sophisticated and highly advanced in technology and social interaction both good and unfortunately, evil. They retain most of their animal physical characteristics but were propelled into a much higher degree of erudition by a near catastrophic explosion on their sun. Homo Sapiens once populated their world but succumbed in the blast. Now these super beasts dominate. You will be introduced to several of them shortly if you decide to take on the mission the Queen has in mind. You and your associates come from Earth Beta. You will be asked to work with Sherlock Holmes once again. Earth Alpha is over a century ahead of you in time and thousands of light years away. "

"Light years, Raymond?"

"Copernicus, please explain!"

"Milady. Light travels at a fixed rate of speed. 186,000 miles per second; 671 million miles per hour."

"Goodness, How swift! I wish Pookie and I could flit that fast. I never thought of that. Did you, Sisi? Mr. Sherman? I'm sure Galileo and DaVinci know all about it. But what's a light year? Is it the same as an Earth year? We are eternal here in Heaven so not everybody bothers to think about it."

St. Catherine of Alexandria shook her head sadly and sighed.

Copernicus continued. "A light year actually measures distance not time. A light-year is the expanse over which light travels in 365.25 Earth Beta days. 5.88 trillion miles with a 't'."

"And you say this world you want us to visit is thousands of these light years away from our Earth? Well, I guess a miracle or two is called for."

"Not really a miracle, Baroness. The angels do it all the time."

"Now, there's a point. Why does the Queen want us to go if she can send angels?"

"She wants someone with a history of mortality and foibles."

"Well, that's certainly me. Who am I meeting and what's the mission?"

"She'll tell you when we finish this tutorial. Now one very important item. As I said, there are no Homo Sapiens on this world you'll be visiting. Its dominant population are animals similar to the ones on your former world and in Mr. Sherman's Meadows. But they are as highly sentient and intelligent as you and me or maybe even more so. Look at this presentation."

An image of a large brown bear shimmered in the celestial atmosphere. His demeanor was solemn. His voice was deep and rumbling. He was lecturing to an unseen audience.

"About 100,000 years ago, according to scientific experts, a colossal solar flare blasted out from our Sun, creating gigantic magnetic storms here on our Earth Alpha. These highly charged electrical tempests caused startling physical and psychological imbalances in the then population of our world.

The complete nervous systems of some species were totally destroyed. For example, Homo Sapiens lost all mental and motor capabilities and rapidly became extinct.

Less developed species exposed to the radiation were affected differently. Four-footed and finned mammals, birds and reptiles suddenly found themselves capable of complex thought, enhanced emotions, self-awareness, social consciousness and the ability to communicate, sometimes orally, sometimes telepathically, often both. Both speech production and speech perception slowly progressed with the evolution of tongues, lips, vocal cords and enhanced ear to brain connections. Many species developed opposable digits, fingers or claws, further accelerating civilized progress. Some others (most fish and underground dwellers) were shielded from radiation and remained only as sentient as they were before the blast. This event is referred to as The Big Shock. It remains under intensive study.

Furthermore, in the knowledge that we are not alone in the cosmos, my staff and I are heavily engaged in Project Multiverse, successful searches for alternate universes, especially those in which Homo Sapiens continues to live and hopefully, prospers."

The speech ended, the vision disappeared and Copernicus remarked, "That was Octavius Bear Ph.D. quoting from his *Our Origins on Earth Alpha*, a section in his "An Introduction to Faunapology."

The Baroness and her colleagues were amazed. "An incredibly articulate bear with a Ph.D.! Are they all like that?"

Copernicus replied, "No, He's a genius and very rich and powerful but most of the animals on Earth Alpha are quite similar in knowledge, capability, emotions and relationships to those of us who came from Earth Beta."

"And the Queen wants us to join this Octavius Bear and do what?"

Raymond smiled, "As soon as this session is over, you can ask her yourself."

*****

A magnificent glass tower imposes itself on the sky at one end of the Elysian Fields reflecting the rays of the eternal sun. *(At the other end stands the endless Cosmic Cathedral and the palaces of the Almighty.)* This is the Celestial Executive Complex. Here Heavenly Real Estate runs its offices under St. Joseph's direction. The Managing Committee meets periodically within its chambers. Angelic Transport has its command center and garages for its chariots at the base of the building. Celestial Communications controls its networks from its studios and offices. At the pinnacle sits the administrative headquarters of Her Majesty, Mary, Queen of Heaven.

Director Raymond, Lady Juliet, Mr. Sherman, Empress Sisi and Pookie flitted into a large golden anteroom where a group of angels were busily watching screens and directing activities.

One of the angels rose and greeted the group. Orifiel, the Baroness' former Guardian Angel. He fluttered his graceful wings, smiled *(beatifically of course)* and said, "Greetings and blessings on you all. Welcome to Angelic Central. The administrative and clerical hub supporting Her Majesty's numerous responsibilities. It is good to see you again, Lady Juliet. And welcome, Empress Sisi, Mr. Sherman and of course, Pookie. Director

Raymond, the Queen will be with you shortly. Right now, she is appearing to a group of pilgrims in Africa."

"Oh. Orifiel. How wonderful to see you again. You seem to have risen in the Angelic ranks."

Director Raymond chuckled. "After being your guardian for so many earth years, he deserved a promotion."

The Baroness blushed, "Orifiel, was I really that difficult to guide?"

"There were moments, Milady. Ah, Her Majesty has returned. One moment and I'll announce you.

The simple door to her office opened and the Queen of Heaven emerged. "No need for formalities, Orifiel. I have met these people and dog before. Come in, come in! Welcome to my work room." She stood aside in the passageway, dressed in a plain blue robe with no jewelry, decorations or crown to proclaim her rank. Her gracious smile showed in both her mouth and sparkling eyes. Her perfect Semitic profile and complexion confirmed her agelessness.

The chamber was large and sun-filled. A sizeable desk-like piece of furniture was centered in front of the radiant windows. *(A gift from her carpenter Son.)* Several large display screens floated above its surface, each showing different forms of brisk activity. Subdued celestial music played in the background. She sat and gestured toward a cluster of chairs surrounding her table and asked them to join her. One chair was already occupied by another Semitic woman resting serenely in a brown robe with two rings on her fingers and a bracelet of carnelian gem stones. All this set off by her striking long red hair and flawless face.

The Queen smiled and stretched her arm out to the woman and said, "Let me introduce another Mary. Mary Magdalene. We call her Magda. Two thousand Earth Beta years ago many Jewish women bore the name Mary. Most confusing!" Magda smiled as the Queen made the introductions.

Juliet said, "Your Majesty…'

The Queen interrupted. "No formality required. I shall be Mary and you shall be Juliet. Magda is Magda and you Empress, shall be Sisi. Mr. Sherman, your name is Alec, is it not?"

The zoologist nodded his head in agreement still taken aback with her presence.

While all this was going on, Pookie climbed up on the Queen's lap and curled into a white curly ball. Juliet gestured for the dog to get down but Mary laughed and scratched the canine between her ears. "Stay, Pookie. Thank goodness, you're not one of those Lipizzaner stallions. I'd be buried."

Sisi giggled. "I've come close several times."

Mary smiled again. She scanned the screens floating in front of her. "Orifiel, there seems to be some extra activity at Angelic Central. Would you look into it, please? Meanwhile, let's begin our discussion. I assume you're curious about why you are here."

Juliet chuckled, "Me? Curious? Never!"

Mary didn't return her laugh. "Oh yes, you are! Actually. That's one of the reasons I asked you to come. You may remember I designated you a Marian Agent. That was not a casual decision. You have a history of solving crimes and pursuing malefactors. You and that Sherlock Holmes."

"Holmes is the professional. I'm his very junior partner."

"Well, very junior partner, I have an assignment for you and for the moment, it can't involve Sherlock Holmes. Not until you have dealt with the preliminaries. Raymond, I assume Juliet has been m ade aware of the existence of Earth Alpha and its sentient animal denizens. More to the point, she has been exposed to Doctor Octavius Bear."

"She has, madam."

The Baroness retorted. "If listening to a giant bear talk remotely about his world's history and characteristics for thirty seconds constitutes exposure, I suppose I have been. I still don't know what this is all about." Pookie sat up in the Queen's lap and whined. Mary patted her.

"Yes, dear. We shall see that you and your mistress are fully briefed. Throughout the universe, hundreds of billions of creatures are undergoing oppression, deprivation, pain and cruelty. My Son showed great compassion for them to the point of dying on a cross on their behalf. Many of them are here in the limitless realms of heaven finding their rewards after suffering from petty tyrants, greedy plutocrats and social neglect. Satan controls some of these environments and situations. Lady Juliet, you have met Satan and know whereof I speak. This is the Kingdom of Heaven that so many aspire to. Satan tries his best to prevent them from entering. The battle goes on."

Meanwhile, Orifiel had returned. "A minor misunderstanding, Your Majesty. Things are back to perfection again."

"Thank you, Orifiel. Juliet, listen carefully."

"There is a major issue that will affect both Earths very shortly to the catastrophic extent of total destruction. Heaven seldom intervenes directly in the affairs of mortals but this time the Almighty has decided to do so. They have given the task to me and Magda to resolve. If you choose to accept it, this will be your mission, Juliet. First, secure the cooperation of Octavius Bear and his team, the Octavians. After gaining the confidence of the animals on Earth Alpha you will be free to involve Sherlock Holmes on Earth Beta. At the moment, he does not believe other worlds exist. It's up to you and Octavius to convince him and secure his assistance. But first you must meet this formidable Bear and get his cooperation."

"Why us? I would think an angel or a ghostly spirit from Earth Alpha would be more appropriate to work with this Octavius. Goodness knows there are plenty of them in their own section of Paradise."

"You're correct. Angels are our usual messengers and warriors. We could send an archangel or two to resolve the problem. But in this case we prefer ex-mortals with experience in dealing with uncontrolled criminals. Sherlock Holmes, Octavius Bear and you fit that description. Octavius is a highly experienced criminologist and has been exposed to 'homo sapiens' in his quantum travels on exoplanets. He is disposed to work with them. Holmes, as you well know, has dealt with evil doers for decades. We will have Orifiel and other guardian angels with you at all times to assist you. Being immortal, you will be in no physical or psychic danger but you may not succeed. Empress Sisi and Alec? Will you serve as backups to the Baroness and her associates?"

Sisi nodded. "This sounds very exciting."

Mr. Sherman said, "If any animals are harmed, I and my staff will be ready to assist."

Mary turned to Juliet and asked, "Well, will you accept the assignment?'

"Of course, Your Majesty. But first, I'd like to know. What do you want me to do?"

"Magda, please enlighten the team. Ensure they have full knowledge of what we expect."

Mary Magdalene had been silent up to this point. She frowned. "As the Queen has said, No harm will come to you but you will be engaged in preventing the destruction of most of the populations of two worlds. Earths Alpha and Beta. A madman known to Sherlock Holmes is plotting cosmic conquest. To do that he plans to eliminate all but the beings he chooses to make his slaves. His name is Professor James Moriarty. Holmes believes he is dead.

He is not. Octavius is unfamiliar with him. Your first task is to make him aware of the man and the threat,"

Juliet returned the frown. "I have heard of Moriarty. The Super Criminal! Holmes referred to him as the Napoleon of Crime. Holmes and Watson think he is dead. You say he's still alive and active in both worlds. How does he have access to Earth Alpha? Raymond and Copernicus say Alpha is over a century ahead of Beta in time and thousands of light years away."

Magda replied. "There is a process that deals with that issue called Quantum Travel. It's not yet available to your Earth Beta and only in highly restricted use in Earth Alpha. Octavius Bear and his associates are experts in its practice. So, too, to a lesser degree, is an erratic horse named General Turmoil. He is head of a secret organization called The Business. He also has ambitions of world conquest. The General looked back in history and space and found Moriarty. He quantum transited to your former world and proposed a partnership. A Horse and Homo Sapiens. Together they would conquer both Earths. Two of the most sophisticated and advanced exoplanets in the Universe. This would only be the first step for the Professor. Moriarty wants to conquer the entire Cosmos as he understands it. Their plan calls for widespread destruction and subjugation of both worlds leaving only a population of submissive slaves. They are plotting and gathering weapons and other military resources on a third deserted but livable exoplanet. They must be stopped in short order before they have a chance to carry out their horrific plans. First Octavius and then Holmes must be informed and spurred to action. Your job!"

Juliet sucked in her ethereal breath. "All right, Mary and Magda, but I'll need far more information including how to do this quantum jumping."

Raymond raised his hand. "My job! Come and we'll get you and your dog briefed and prepared. Empress Sisi and Mr. Sherman, you come too. Lead on, Orifiel."

Mary rose and gave her blessing to the party. "I know you will succeed. The Almighty is watching over you, too."

Sisi looked at Mr. Sherman, shrugged her shoulders and said, "Being friends with the Baroness has meant one adventure after another. You and I are in for some exciting times."

He shook his head. "I thought keeping track and caring for animals was challenging. Little did I know."

As they left the room, Juliet could be heard humming, "Heigh-ho, heigh-ho, to other worlds we go!" Punctuated by canine barks.

Chapter Two

In a conference room in Angelic Central, Juliet, Pookie, Magda, Sisi, Mr. Sherman, Director Raymond and Orifiel sat around a large table.

The Baroness asked, "Orifiel, have you been to Earth Alpha?"

"Oh yes, Milady. We guardian angels serve all worlds. We work to guide and protect sentient and non-sentient beings in all the exoplanets wherever there are. They are all God's creatures. Of course, some of them are without much moral or social judgment. Some are atheists. Some claim they have no souls. Not so! They are often quite different. Earth Alpha and Earth Beta were much alike until that sun explosion you heard Octavius Bear mention. Then Homo Sapiens, your species, died out and was replaced by the sentient animals you will meet shortly. Alpha is ahead of your native world in technical and social development by close to 125 Earth years. Much will be new, unfamiliar and even shocking to you. However, many basics remain the same. Good and evil, cleverness and stupidity, grace and clumsiness, beauty and ugliness, senselessness and good judgment. This horse, General Turmoil and Professor Moriarty are from different worlds but share deep desires for conquest. They are only the latest versions. As you know, would-be conquerors and dictators have existed from all time."

"True, but never with ambitions on such a cosmic scale."

Magdalene replied. "Indeed! That is why they must be stopped but by living mortal beings. Octavius Bear and Sherlock Holmes. Angels, saints and spirits such as you and I may guide and assist but those two have been designated to be the primary actors in this drama. Bear against Horse, Human against Human. They already have a long history. Now, Orifiel, let's take these spirits through an Earth Alpha familiarization briefing."

"Certainly madam! Baroness, a lot has happened in 125 years on Alpha. Most of it will take place on Beta as well but not necessarily in exactly the same way or sequence. Let's start with technology. Octavius Bear and his cohorts are scientific geniuses."

Much later! Juliet was overwhelmed. "My goodness. Passenger and cargo airplanes, huge powered ships, high speed trains, automobiles, radio, television, computers, this thing called the Internet, Artificial Intelligence, *(I'm fascinated by these units called Ursulas!)* super-sized warships, and unfortunately highly destructive weapons. Rockets and space exploration. H.G.Wells and Jules Verne would be amazed. New drugs and medical processes and equipment. Longer lives. Females not only with the vote but leading many countries. Children getting a lengthy formal education. But there are still slaves and crime and violence. Animals against animals. Jean-Baptiste Alphonse Karr had it right. *'Plus ça change, plus c'est la même chose.'* The more things change, the more they stay the same. All right, Orifiel. Let's take an inter-stellar flit."

"Here, Pookie. Come to momma. We're off to see the Octavian wizards." Whoosh!

*****

Momentary blackness and whistling winds followed by a gentle touchdown. Juliet looked around her. Orifiel was standing next to her and Pookie had jumped down from her arms. They were standing in a huge sunlit

19

area next to what looked like a wide and extensive roadway. A nearby river not unlike the Thames ran slowly in front of some woods. A paddle boat was tied up on the shoreline. Several enormous structures surrounded her. A very substantial five storey white marble mansion, with large French windows and balconies took up the center of the area. *(almost as spectacular as her own heavenly abode)* Next to it stood a cavernous gold and white Roman Temple, flanked by an Asiatic pagoda that would have done Confucius proud.

A large birdlike machine in blue, gold and white sat on an open paved space. The printing on the side said 'Aquabear.' Further back a series of letters and numbers ran to what looked like a metal tail. Unseen by the mortals, a group of guardian angels stood in the background. Several animals were busy with the machine. Pookie rushed over to them but being invisible, she made no impression. However, one large dog, a Husky, sniffed the air surrounding her. He sensed something.

"Where are we, Orifiel? Who are these animals?"

"In order of their size and dimensions, Baroness, we are on Earth Alpha, North America, the United States, an area called Greater Cincinnati on the Ohio River at the headquarters of Octavius Bear in the Alpha year 2040. This place is called the Bear's Lair. Those animals are some of the Bear's associates and employees. One of his homes and headquarters is in that grand mansion you see. *(They have another center in the Shetland Islands in Scotland.)* This one goes many levels deep into the ground where he has his laboratories, offices and communication center. He owns a very substantial business called Universal Ursine Industries (UUI) headquartered across the river in Kentucky and a massive technical complex called the Deep Data Super

Computing Center at the Hexagon further west. That's where those Ursulas you're so interested in are developed. He and his wife are incredibly wealthy. As you saw during our briefing, he is an expert in many disciplines, including criminology."

"That Roman temple has no religious significance. It houses the flying machines belonging to the Bear and his consort, Bearoness Belinda Béarnaise Bruin Bear (nee Black)."

"She is a widowed member of Scottish nobility and called a Bearoness for obvious reasons. She's a highly sentient, clever and very wealthy Polar Bear and yes, you share many characteristics. Like you, she spent many years in show business. She as an aqua star, you as a musical performer. She is the owner of an opulent resort in the Shetlands and shares much of your UK background. She was married to a feckless Scottish Bearon, now deceased. She is the mother of twin hybrid juveniles, Arabella and McTavish. Like their parents, they are brilliant. I am sure you and Bearoness Belinda will be quite simpatico."

"A Baroness by marriage, like me?"

"Perhaps I should appear to her first. Is she here?"

"I don't know if she is in residence. I shall find out. I suspect she arrived recently on that flying machine you see there. It is called a Concorde SST, a supersonic airplane."

"Supersonic airplane?"

"Yes, it flies through the air at speeds in excess of the speed of sound. About 760 miles per hour. Not quite flitting speed but you don't have to be disembodied to achieve it. Speaking of disembodied, I'm sure you know that you and Pookie are permitted to become corporeal at will. I and the other angels cannot but I will be here to assist you in any way I can."

"For goodness sakes, stay nearby. Let's see if we can find this Bearoness."

Pookie was curious and had gone about her investigations, searching out these remarkable animals. Mr. Sherman would be delighted to meet them. She wondered how Der Alte and the rest of the Lipizzaner stallions would react. What about Pegasus and the Unicorn? Were there any horses here? There certainly seemed to be dogs and oh my, a pair of wolves standing next to that Concorde winged thing. She didn't need a flying machine. She could aviate on her own. After all, she was an Honor member of the True Angels aerobatic team back in Heaven.

She looked back and saw her mistress moving toward the big mansion. Now what? She trotted over and joined Juliet and the angel as they approached the structure. That large attractive Husky dog was standing in the huge doorway. She needed to materialize and get acquainted with him. But right now they had to find this Bearoness. Funny, she'd never seen a Polar Bear before. In fact, there were several species she was unacquainted with even with her frequent visits to the Meadows. This would soon be rectified.

She'd have more wild stories to share with her canine companions in the Meadows the next time they got together for a game of Multi-Dimensional

Fetch. And of course, there were the horses. They'd be fascinated by the fact that one of the villains of this piece was an evil military horse.

Pookie wasn't sure what all this to-ing and fro-ing was all about. Something about conquering worlds and enslaving their denizens. That she could understand. She'd been with the Baroness and Sherlock Holmes often enough to know how evil some people could be. Was it the same with these animals? Did they know about heaven, the saints, angels and Queen Mother? Did they even know about God? The dog may be non-verbal but she had a highly intelligent head on her shoulders enhanced by her heavenly nature. She could also fly, flit and flip as well as hold her own in a dogfight. No one was going to put one over on Pookie. She was ready to support Lady Juliet yet again. She growled menacingly and trotted off after the Baroness and angel.

"Pookie, come along, dear. We have to visit this Bearoness and her consort. They and their companions have a great history of successfully battling criminals and 'ne'er-do-wells.' Queen Mary wants them to join with Sherlock Holmes and Watson in defeating Professor Moriarty and a terrible horse named General Turmoil. We both have major experience with wonderful horses but this one is a fiend. They want to enslave the Universe."

The dog recognized evil when she heard it. This sounded serious. Something for Heaven's Top Gun to take on. Baroness Juliet, Sherlock Holmes, Watson and Pookie. A formidable team. But who were these Octavian animals? Were they as good as the stories about them made them out to be? Pookie was a bit dubious but she'd give them the benefit of the doubt.

Chapter Three

The angel and two ghosts flitted inside the mansion passing the handsome butler dog standing in the massive doorway. He turned and strode inside the lobby. They flitted through the opulent interior, taking in the décor as they moved. Top of the line! Ornate splendor! Juliet was impressed.

They entered an extensive lounge with randomly scattered tables and couches. Wood paneling and sparkling chandeliers with nature prints lining the walls. Sounds of laughter, clinking glass bowls and voices tinged with squeaks and growls. The butler and a maid re-entered carrying sandwiches, cakes and drinks on trays. Several gorgeous female animals were lying on couches in varied positions with bowls of some liquid, probably alcoholic, in their paws. The girls! "Les Elegantes!" Sitting and standing on the far side of the room were four invisible Guardian Angels keeping close watch over their respective charges. Orifiel bowed to them and received waves in return.

A large white polar bear dominated the group. Holding court! She was beautiful! Her facial structure was perfect and her body spoke of years of careful discipline. This was no doubt, Bearoness Belinda Béarnaise Bruin Bear (nee Black). A small tiara crowned her head, a gold necklace rested on her fur and sapphire earrings dangled from her small but well-shaped ears. And, oh yes, an ankle bracelet! Lady Juliet shared her enthusiasm for fashion and tasteful jewelry. Clearly, a current or former member of the aristocracy and theatre. She recalled from her briefing that the Bearoness was once the diving and swimming star of a water review troupe called The Aquabears. A famous showbear.

Seated nearby was a lovely grey she-wolf with a marvelously voluminous tail, lean body and beautiful face. Her eyes flashed and her ears perked up during the conversation. Not a glamor-girl. She was a formidable warrior. Next to her and chirping in an enthusiastic fashion was a cheetah. Her long legs and tail seemed to stretch on forever and she wore a large diamond choker around her neck. Her tawny pelt was covered with spots with a white underbelly. Her head was small and rounded, with a short snout and black tear-like facial streaks. They were both gorgeous animals.

Pookie was taken aback with the next member. A Bichon Frisé! They could have been twin sisters except this one was a bit smaller and wearing a small turban between her ears. Not a halo like hers.

Unseen, Lady Juliet, the angel and Pookie were listening to the conversations. The Baroness was relieved to note that all of Les Elegantes, as she nicknamed them, spoke a version of English that was comprehensible. Each had their own accent. Belinda spoke a broad American even though she was a Scottish Bearoness. The wolf had a Germanic or Swiss inflection. The Bichon spoke with insertions of French. The cheetah was most peculiar. She growled and purred in a definite US accent but when she was excited, she chirped in what sounded for all the world like London Cockney. This required further study. Juliet would be able to get by with her posh Mayfair voice – she had spent lots of time among the toffs and ended up being one herself. Plus she could always invoke the Heavenly Universal Language privilege that allowed all Paradise denizens to communicate with each other regardless of their original nationality and dialects.

Belinda was speaking. "Well, that trip from Polar Paradise was a bit wearing but I love to pilot the Aquabear. Chita, are you OK. I know you're not crazy about flying."

The cheetah was nodding off. Jet lag even after a supersonic flight.

The Polar turned to the French Bichon and asked, "Where has Maury got you and Otto booked next, Giselle?"

"Ooh, Lala! Would you believe television? Mais oui! Prime time, no less! The studio's in New York."

"Well, we'll have to fly you up there." She turned to the she-wolf. "Frau Schuylkill. Are you up for a trip to the Big Apple?"

She nodded. "Of course. Anything for my little friend and her crazy cohort, Otto the idiot otter."

The French Bichon growled, "He's not an idiot. He's a very talented slapstick artist and a highly skilled warrior. He's Sir Otto the Magnificent knighted by the Merow of Orb."

This remark struck Juliet. The Merow of Orb. Yet another exoplanet. She needed to get further informed on all these cosmic locations. They might have a bearing (no pun) on her mission. She decided that this wasn't the moment to materialize. She would wait until the Bearoness was alone. She looked at Pookie. "Not yet, dear! You can meet your Bichon counterpart and that hunky Husky a little later. I need to make the Bearoness' acquaintance without causing a riot."

She had picked up the ladies' names. The Bearoness was Belinda. The Cheetah was called Chita. Not very original but accurate enough. The Wolf was Frau Schuylkill – German or Swiss. The Bichon was Madame Giselle but Juliet and Pookie both suspected the name was theatrical.

Belinda yawned and said, "I'm sorry but I am beat. Old age is catching up with me. You should be tired too, Chita. I'm heading off for a nap. Octavius should be showing up shortly. He, Maury and the Twins are coming back from Australia on the Ursa Major. They were down with Bruce Wallaroo on some case or other."

She headed to the elevator leading up to the family suites on the fourth floor. Pookie scampered on ahead and sat by the door waiting for the car to descend. Juliet and Orifiel joined her and when it arrived they slipped inside the lift along with the Bearoness. Joining them was the Bearoness' Guardian Angel – Dara. He/she *(angels have no gender)* greeted them and welcomed them to the Bear's Lair. Like all of the celestials, the angel could usually only be seen and heard by other immortals. They emerged in a luxurious anteroom and Belinda glided into the equally sumptuous bedroom, taking off her tiara, necklace and earrings.

The bedroom's lavish appointments matched the opulent character of the entire mansion. Actually, it was three rooms in one. Plush gold carpeting. A sitting area with comfortable recliners, tables, TV, computers and stereo. Desktop telephones, sideboards and a large refrigerator. Crystal decanters and glasses sparkled in the light of chandeliers and pin spots. An enormous bedroom befitting the size of its ursine residents with an emperor size bed, multiple wardrobes, Rococo end tables, chaises longues, antique lamps, gold silk drapes, vases filled with wildflowers and a large wall size television. The ensuite bath was a mini-spa complete with jacuzzies and enormous tubs.

A large laptop computer and virtual reality headset sat on a desk in the sitting room. The Bearoness spoke to it. She addressed it as Ursula. "I'm going to take a nap, Ursula. Wake me if Octavius arrives or any other major event crops up." The machine rang a chime in response. Juliet's curiosity was piqued. She needed to find out more about this wonderful device. Obviously they were products of Octavius Bear's technical empire. But what could they do? Who makes them and where? She wanted to see one up close and possibly interact with it.

Before Belinda got a chance to flop on the oversized bed and its satin sheets, Juliet and Pookie materialized. Orifiel stayed invisible. The dog snuffled. Belinda looked in the direction of the noise, spotted the dog and said, "Hello, little one, you look just like Giselle. Who are you? Where did you come from?"

Then she realized a beautiful dark haired female Homo Sapiens in a scarlet gown was standing behind the canine. Unshaken, the Polar sow had met H. Saps before on her trips to the exoplanets, specifically Gaea. She addressed the 'woman.' *(Wasn't that what they were called?)* "Who are <u>you?</u> Where did <u>you</u> come from?"

"Forgive the intrusion, Bearoness Belinda. I am Lady Juliet Armstrong, Baroness Crestwell formerly of Earth Beta. More recently, from the heavenly realm." She blinked out momentarily. Pookie did likewise. When they both returned, they were sporting their haloes and as usual, the dog's was askew.

Belinda was unphased and chuckled, "A spectral noblewoman. Well, that's a new one on me. And a ghost dog. What is your name, sweetheart?"

Pookie barked and did a backflip. "Well, you're certainly talented but I take it you don't talk. Is that correct, Lady Juliet?"

"Yes, she's an Earth Beta canine. Smart as a whip but nonverbal. Her name is Pookie. She was my pet when we were both alive and now we're partners again in the spirit world. You don't seem taken aback by being addressed by ghosts."

"When you live with Octavius Bear, you're prepared for anything. What brings you to the Bear's Lair? Are you truly a Baroness of the British Realm on Earth Beta?"

"Since I am dead, I suppose I am a Baroness Emeritus or Expired. I lead a rather interesting afterlife in Paradise."

Belinda laughed. "So do I. In Polar Paradise. It's my castle/resort in the Shetlands. I share it with my husband and a group of associates we call the Octavians and a massive number of cold-loving tourists. I'm American but a Scottish Bearoness by a former marriage. "

"I'd love to visit it and meet your colleagues. I am most interested in meeting Doctor Bear. I am here on a vital mission that we hope will involve him and the rest of you as well."

"Oh dear! Octavius and I are supposed to be retired but we never seem to be able to pull it off. If you're from Heaven, I assume it's a directive from the Almighty? Surely, you're not on Satan's side."

"Absolutely not! But I've met him. Not a pleasant experience! Actually, my commission comes from Mary the Queen of Heaven acting on behalf of the Trinity. A truly wonderful woman. I hope you get to meet her someday"

"Well, I'd have to die to do that but that's inevitable and I'd have to go to Heaven and that is definitely not inevitable."

"I suspect that accepting this mandate will help tremendously. I'm still not sure why I was admitted to Paradise. By the way, we both share a show business background. You are a world famous aqueuse. I was a star of the London musical theatre before I married and was shot."

"Shot? Oh, I had assumed you died of natural causes."

"Not unless you regard a rifle bullet as natural. Pookie predeceased me and waited outside the Rainbow Bridge until I appeared. But I told the Heavenly Authorities I wouldn't venture inside the Pearly Gates until I found out who killed me and delivered them to justice. They grudgingly agreed. I enlisted Sherlock Holmes as a partner in my search. He was reluctant at first but we are now often together fighting yet another criminal."

The polar opened her eyes wide. "Sherlock Holmes? So he really exists. Octavius will be fascinated."

"He not only exists but part of my directive is to get the two of them together to foil a nefarious cosmic plot involving both Earths."

"Oh my! Intriguing! I can't wait for him to arrive so you can share your story. Meanwhile, let me invite you to share our hospitality. Do you consume earthly food and drink?"

"Yes and no. When we materialize, we can enjoy your edibles and beverages. Pookie is addicted to Heavenly Chewies, an animal snack from the Angelic Kitchens."

"I'd like to introduce you to our associates but perhaps I should wait for Octavius to get here."

"Yes, please do. I want to explain my mission to the two of you and then you can choose what you want to do and whom you want to enlighten. Meanwhile, a glass of champagne would go down very nicely."

"Agreed. I'll send down for a bottle of Belanger Cuvee. I was going to take a nap but you have me fascinated. Pookie, come sit on the couch with me" The dog did her signature backflip and bounced up on the couch. With her white fur, she disappeared into the Bearoness' massive side with only her black nose and intense eyes showing. Juliet fed her one more of her tasty tidbits. The angel Dara sat by, watching and listening carefully.

*****

The roar of huge jet engines echoed over the Ohio River as the massive C5A approached the faux Interstate Highway extension that served as the runway for the Bear's Lair. Not really a public artery, local authorities looked the other way and construction equipment moved about in simulated building activities to maintain the image of ongoing development. The Great Bear could afford to keep up the illusion.

Up in the cockpit, two white Bengals were going through their landing procedure checklists. Benedict and Galatea Tigris. Ben and Gal! Bengal? Known as the Flying Tigers, they piloted the Great Bear's and Bearoness' aircraft. There were other pilots among the Octavians. The she-wolf, Frau Schuylkill and her mate Colonel Wyatt Where and of course, the Bearoness herself. Belinda delighted in flying the Aquabear, her Concorde SST, in which she had recently arrived from the Shetlands.

Back in the body of the enormous airplane, the Ursa Major, Octavius was stretched out in a comfortable pod suited to his nine foot frame. Because of his narcolepsy brought on by his self-induced genetic modifications to avoid having to hibernate, the Great Bear could not drive, run machinery, pilot boats or aircraft. He paid a very capable staff to do that for him in addition to his wife. Snoozing in a plush seat nearby, Mauritius Meerkat (Maury) his two foot tall sidekick, was unaware of their impending arrival. On the opposite side sat Arabella and McTavish, hybrid offspring of Octavius and Belinda. They were a brilliant pair reflecting their parents' spectacular genes and had become world famous for their sensationally successful electronic games. They were, as usual, working away at their next offering, *Bears in the Air* with help from an Ursula Artificial General Intelligence (AGI) system and a hookup to the Deep Data Super Computing Center at the Hexagon in Kentucky. Unseen but actively aware, four Guardian Angels were sequestered in the rear.

They were all returning from an engagement in Australia with Chief Inspector Bruce Wallaroo and Private Detective Tilda Roo tackling a ring of international smugglers of weapons and parts. The military cabal was broken up, the booty recovered and the leaders were on their way to The Defence Force Correctional Establishment (DFCE) at Holsworthy

Barracks in Sydney, New South Wales. The twins were working up scenarios of the caper for their games. Now it was time to return to the Bear's Lair. Octavius had hoped to finally start his retirement but he couldn't have turned down the request from his Aussie pal. Maybe now, he'd get the chance. He'd have to sit down and plan once more with Belinda.

A deep feline voice came over the ship's intercom reciting the time-honored "fasten seat belts and secure all loose objects" commands. They were heading in. Octavius nudged Maury, waking him from his deep sleep. The sounds of lowering flaps, descending landing gear, change of pitch in the engines, a solid thump, roaring thrust reversers and the Ursa Major started her roll toward the mansion and Roman temple where a ground crew and committee of greeters awaited the international travelers.

*****

In the family suite, Belinda's acute hearing picked up the sounds of the landing plane. She turned to Juliet and said, "Apologies, Baroness but my husband, children and their associate have just arrived. I must go and welcome them home."

The ghost smiled and said, "Would you mind if I accompanied you, invisibly of course? Pookie and I will await your invitation to solidify."

"Certainly, come along. Although I think I'll want to introduce you to Tavi before you reveal yourselves to the others. "

"I'm not sure we should disclose our presence to your team before we have a chance to discuss our mission with you two. Octavius may not be willing to take on the assignment. You may not either."

"Knowing my husband, I think he will but we'll see. Let's go down to the entrance."

The Baroness and her dog disappeared after signaling to Orifiel and Dara to join them. The angels shrugged their wings into full array and flew down behind them to the oversized doorway. They flitted outside past Huntley, the Husky butler and another staff animal just as the jet stairs of the huge transport lowered and two juvenile hybrid bears skittered down to the tarmac. They spotted Belinda coming through the mansion's entranceway and rushed to hug her. "Hi, Mom. We're back from Oz. What a great trip! Dad, Inspector Bruce and Miss Tilda got the military case all wrapped up and the bad guys are in jail. We're putting the whole thing in a new game. What's to eat?"

"I'm sure Frau Schuylkill has some wonder snacks waiting to you in the kitchen."

"Great!" They raced through the door slapping Huntley on his well-shaped flank as they went. "Hi, Huntley! We're back."

"Yes, Mr. McTavish. I noticed. Welcome home! The Frau has prepared some treats for you."

"Good! We're starved."

Juliet chuckled as the two whirlwinds disappeared into the mansion. She looked over and noticed a meerkat, short of body, long of tail, advancing slowly from the plane, yawning vehemently in the process.

Bearoness Belinda hugged the suricate and said, "Maury. You look beat. Intercontinental jet lag? Come on in. The gang is waiting for you, the Twins and Octavius. Where is he?"

No sooner had she asked when a nine foot, brown Kodiak descended the cargo ramp at the tail of the aircraft. He pawsed and waved and then continued down the slope to the asphalt circle. Behind him, the four guardian angels, invisible to the mortals, flitted to the ground from the plane.

Juliet looked at Pookie and said, "There he is, Miss Dog. Our Cosmic hero. Let's hope he's in the mood to take up our request."

The dog whined and scratched her ear.

Belinda and Octavius stood erect in a classic bear hug. The Great Bear snorted. "Glad to be back, Bel. Well, that mess is settled. Bruce owes me one but I must admit it was a worthwhile trip. The Twins are already adding it to their latest game, I'll tell you all about it later. What's new?"

"Funny you should ask. We have guests. Get yourself a drink and I'll introduce you"

"Guests? I don't remember extending any invitations."

"No. They descended out of the blue."

Juliet, Orifiel and Dara laughed. "How true! How true!" She looked up as the two Flying Tigers exited the pilot's hatch with their guardian angels and proceeded to talk with the ground crew. A tug attached a spar to the nose gear and proceeded to pull the huge craft toward the Roman Temple.

Octavius waved at Galatea and Benedict and shouted. "Thanks, team. Great flight as usual." The white Bengals waved back.

Baroness Juliet looked at Orifiel. "That's a formidable pair. These Octavians are a group I'd be glad to have on my side. Let's hope they're up to taking on this crazy Horse and the Professor."

The angel nodded and Pookie gave out a soundless bark. Dara flitted over to the angels who had just exited the plane and brought one over. A genderless celestial being suitably matched to Octavius' nine foot height with massive iridescent wings, he/she bowed to the Baroness and said, "I am Adriel, Guardian Angel of Octavius Bear. I am pleased to meet you, Lady Juliet. Dara and I shall be happy to assist you in performing the Queen's mission. Guiding the Great Bear is a formidable task. He is quite capable of getting himself and his group into dangerous situations."

Juliet nodded and returned his bow with a graceful curtsey. The dog did likewise.

Octavius turned to Belinda. "OK! Let me get some mead and you can bring in these mysterious newcomers. I hope this doesn't mean more work. I'm tired. Maury, get yourself a drink and join us. Bel has some unexpected visitors."

The meerkat squinched up his nose and went off in search of a bowl of fermented coconut milk VSOP. The Frau and Huntley had ensured a full supply of potables was available in the lounge for all tastes including soft drinks for the Twins. He poured a substantial shot, took a healthy snort, sighed and suitably armed, headed off to the elevator to the residence suites.

Up in their opulent rooms, Octavius looked around, laughed and said, "Alright, sign in mystery guests!"

To his surprise, a beautiful H.sap woman dressed in a fashionable scarlet gown popped into view. She was holding a Bichon Frisé in her arms. For a moment Tavi thought it was Madame Giselle but he was surprised when the dog wriggled out of her arms, barked, pranced and did a series of back flips. These two were clearly from somewhere else. Probably an exoplanet but how did she do that *'now you don't see me, now you do'* routine.

Belinda giggled, "Surprise! Doctor Octavius Bear, let me introduce Lady Juliet Armstrong, Baroness Crestwell formerly of the Earth Beta United Kingdom, lately of the celestial Kingdom of Heaven. She and her little dog are spirits. They are here on a mission from the Almighty. They want our help. Funny, it's usually the other way around."

"Oh God!" exclaimed Octavius and then sputtered at what he had just said. "Forgive me, Baroness. I've never thought of the Omnipotent as clients. What could I possibly do for them?"

Maury interrupted, "Hold it, Octavius. How do you really know who these two are? They may be aliens from some undiscovered exoplanet who know how to appear and disappear. This stuff about being from the Heavenly Kingdom and on a mission from the Almighty sounds phony to me. Make them prove it."

Belinda frowned and Octavius scratched his head. "I'm sorry. I didn't introduce you to Maury. Mauritius Meerkat is my right paw companion and assistant. He has been with me for ages. I trust his judgment. What you are proposing is well out of the ordinary. He's right. I need some evidence before I get involved with so-called celestial schemes."

Juliet smiled. "Fair enough. I'm not sure I would have believed them if someone showed up with the story I just gave you." She looked at Orifiel who was invisible to the three Octavians and soundlessly asked him. "What do you think, angel? We're going to ask them to engage in some serious business with little or no proof besides our ability to appear and disappear."

Orifiel shook his wings. "Let me contact Director Raymond and see what he says."

The Baroness looked at Belinda and Octavius. "We're arranging for you to be convinced. Just give us a moment. We're bringing in the heavy artillery."

Maury stared at her with a frown. "I'm not sure how you're going to persuade me. Sorry, Baroness or whoever you are. We meerkats aren't very cooperative in the confidence department. My early days with my Mom and Dad taught me to be very alert and suspicious. That's how we survived in the Kalahari Desert in our mob – that's what a family of meerkats is called - mobs or gangs, clans, teams or troops. Then I migrated to Mauritius and took up with a real mob of thieves. I was the lookout and pretty good at it until Octavius here caught me and offered me a chance to work with him or spend a lot of time in an island jail. I've been with him, Belinda and the Octavians ever since - straight as an arrow."

Juliet laughed. "We know your history, Maury. Your guardian angel keeps pretty complete tabs on you." The Meerkat blushed.

Pookie recognized the need for momentary distraction. She skipped over to Maury. They were both about the same size. She flirted, nuzzled him and hopped away, returned and danced on her hind legs and then her forepaws. She repeated the exercise. Finally she executed her signature backflip.

In spite of himself, the meerkat laughed. "Dog, No matter where you're from or who you are, we have to get you together with Madame Giselle and Otto. You'd be a sensational addition to their act."

The Baroness heard this and pondered. Perhaps tying Pookie up with these performers, whoever they were, would help cement relations. Heaven knows, the dog was a wonderful canine artiste who could charm just about anyone. They'd have to meet this Madame Giselle and Otto. She wondered what they did. Her own show business experience wouldn't hurt either.

She looked at Orifiel, Dara and Adriel. They smiled and Dara reached down to pat the dog who having solidified, eluded her angelic touch.

They awaited Director Raymond's arrival. Juliet took another sip of the champagne. Not quite the same as nectar but it was very good. She sometimes missed being mortal but only for very short moments.

Chapter Four

Orifiel signaled Juliet as Director Raymond appeared, causing a mild shock. The Earth Alpha trio found themselves facing an individual who had not been there a moment ago. A middle-aged male, in H.sap form, tall, dressed in morning *(mourning?)* clothes, clean shaven, not a hair out of place, dark eyes, color undetermined. But he seemed to be floating inches above the ground. Mr. Raymond, a Senior Angel and Celestial Director, charged with keeping Paradise in heavenly shape had arrived.

"Greetings Baroness Juliet. Always pleased to see you. And you must be Bearoness Belinda Béarnaise Bruin Bear (nee Black). Enchanted to meet you. A Baroness and Bearoness! Two UK ladyships. And of course the universally famous Octavius Bear. Delighted! Your young Meerkat friend is correct to question the credentials of our emissaries. Now, I am prepared to offer you a quick round trip to Heaven, if you are so inclined. Don't assume that as a result you will eventually pass through the Pearly Gates on your death. That will depend on your worthiness." He winked at Maury. "Having a brief glimpse of Paradise may encourage further improvement of your lifestyle." He turned to Octavius. "I'm sure your suspicious friend here will suggest you don't go. It's entirely up to you. We seldom do this but the mission we will be asking you to undertake is of great import."

Belinda was fascinated with the idea of actually visiting Heaven. She looked at Octavius who was not going to pass up the ultimate adventure either. Maury frowned once again and then simply shrugged. "How do we know you're taking us to Heaven? It could be any fancy exoplanet. You could be kidnappers."

Raymond turned to Belinda. "Your mother Bertha, passed away in an accident on an ice floe. Octavius, your father Jupiter died when you were a cub. And my suspicious friend, not many of your mob back on Mauritius made it to the Elysian Fields but your parents and sister Mabel are with us. You'll meet them all on your short trip. You may regard it as an elaborate trick but that's up to you. By the way, we plan on getting Sherlock Holmes involved in this adventure as well. Mary, the Queen of Heaven and Mary Magdalen want his services joined with yours. After all, we are talking about two different Earths that are in mortal danger."

Octavius snorted, "When are you going to tell us what this so-called mission is all about?'

"As soon as we return and you are convinced that you are dealing with spirits of the celestial afterlife. Now are you prepared for a trip to Paradise? No stairway. We'll flit."

Nods of heads and Belinda, Octavius, Maury, Juliet, Pookie and the invisible Orifiel stood next to Raymond. The Octavians' guardian angels, also unseen, prepared to join them, A wave of the Director's hand and they were off.

*****

The entourage approached the Heavenly Gates instantaneously. Over the Rainbow Bridge and through the Pearly Portals. In the far distance, the Cosmic Cathedral stretched endlessly, Closer by, a magnificent glass-like tower pierced the sky at one end of the Elysian Fields reflecting the rays of the eternal sun. *(At the other end stand the palaces of the Almighty.)*

Raymond spoke. "This is the Celestial Executive Complex. Here Heavenly Real Estate runs its offices under St. Joseph's direction. The Administrative Committee meets periodically within its chambers. The Celestial Command and Communications Center covers the Cosmos constantly updating, directing and assigning the angelic hosts in their countless missions. Angelic Transport has its control center and garages for its chariots at the base of the building. At the pinnacle sits the headquarters of Her Majesty, Mary, Queen of Heaven. Let's enter. She will join us in a moment."

They rose to the top of the tower where a small group of angels sat at golden desks in front of large screens floating in midair. They spoke in musical cadences to invisible entities. Raymond nodded. "Part of the Queen's administrative staff. These are her offices. She occupies that cloud-covered space over there."

Octavius and Belinda were awed. Maury with his quantum travels and theatrical history, thought they were in some kind of spectacular exoplanet theme park. He was astonished but still unconvinced. An amazing place but was it Heaven? Who was this Baroness Juliet and her cute little dog? Doubts persisted.

Suddenly two Semitic H. Sap women appeared. Both beautiful. Both serene. One, dark of hair, was dressed in a subdued blue robe with no symbols to indicate her rank. A gentle smile ringed her mouth and was reflected in her eyes. The other stood in a brown robe with two rings on her fingers and a bracelet of carnelian gem stones. All this set off by her striking long red hair and flawless face. Belinda was glad that she had left most of her Bearonial jewelry back at the Bear's Lair. Humble good taste seemed to be the rule here. Juliet curtsied to the women and Pookie did a graceful bow.

The dark haired woman spoke. "God's Blessings on all of you! Welcome to Heaven or at least its major administrative area. As Lady Juliet and her dog Pookie well know, our celestial domain itself is infinite in size and extent. My name is Mary and I am Heaven's Queen. You may have heard of me and my Son Jesus. This lady is a Mary too. Mary of Magdala. To avoid confusion, I call her Magda. She is my constant companion and spiritual support. Raymond, thank you for bringing these mortals here. Bearoness, Doctor Bear! Your earthly fame has also reached our heavenly domain. Mr. Meerkat, you and the so-called Octavians are also favorably regarded by us as is Mr. Sherlock Holmes, Baroness Juliet's associate. We will be calling on him to assist in this mission we would like you to accept. However, it will be your choice. The Almighty has chosen to give all mortals free will. Magda and I were human once on Earth Beta and made vital decisions of our own. You of course, come from a different world, Earth Alpha, but share all those privileges."

Thus far Belinda and Octavius had said nothing. Maury took it upon himself to reply. "Thank you, Queen Mary but I am puzzled. Why are there no spirits from our world here in what you call Heaven?"

"Ah, but there are, my perceptive but doubting friend, and you shall meet some of them momentarily. A number of other sentient and non-sentient species are here as well. They all have their own heavenly domains, administration and control. We are all free to intermix with each other as you will discover. Many groups are more comfortable staying among their fellows but there is no required segregation. Former H.saps have joined the angels in managing the Almighty's celestial infrastructure but other species actively participate in the conduct of all heavenly affairs. There are no conflicts left unresolved. Come! Magda and Raymond will take you to see some of your deceased family members and fellows. We hope that will convince you that Heaven is real and this is it."

She disappeared and Magda nodded at Raymond. "We are off to see the Earth Alpha contingent. There are many of your predecessors there. Great, good, all saintly and magnificent. All full of joy. You may not be aware but each member of your species had a guardian angel while on Earth Alpha. They were charged with subtly guiding your ancestors to heavenly bliss. Unfortunately, like H.saps and other creatures, not all of them led exemplary lives in spite of angelic urging and protection. While they are not visible, you three, your families and associates have guardian angels constantly watching over you ."

Belinda laughed. "That might well explain how we have survived so many of our – (air quotes) - 'adventures.'

Octavius snorted. "Don't let them get away or go on strike."

"A few of them did rebel once. Have you heard the names Satan, Beelzebub, Astaroth and the term "fallen angels"? Much of the evil in all worlds is initiated and encouraged by them. Lady Juliet, you met Satan and Beelzebub, did you not?"

"Yes! It was not a pleasant experience. I wish none of you ever encounter them."

Raymond said, "Shall we flit to the Earth Alpha sector?"

Belinda looked puzzled, "Flit? There's that word again."

The Director smiled. "Forgive me. I forgot you are not acquainted with our forms of transport. Flitting, as the name suggests, is how we get about for short or medium distances. Of course, we could always summon an angelic chariot."

The Bearoness replied. "I'd like to flit. How do we do it? Maybe we can take a chariot later."

Magda laughed. "There is one shortcoming to the process. You have to be a spirit to do it on your own. Clearly, you have not yet reached that state. However, if Raymond, Juliet and I take your paws, I think we can easily manage it. Perhaps, Mr. Meerkat, given your size, you would be more comfortable flitting with Pookie."

The Bichon barked amiably and offered a paw to Maury. He took it somewhat hesitantly. The others joined appendages. Magda checked them and said, "Wonderful! Let's flit. On to the Earth Alpha's celestial subdivision."

*****

They descended onto a broad park-like plaza intersected by golden paths – each one leading to clusters of shining mansions and villas. Several glowing towers pierced the cloudless sky. The heavenly sun reflected off their white, gold and silver surfaces and a gentle breeze stirred small copses of trees and foliage. Subdued music radiated from nowhere and everywhere. Earth Alpha Celestial Central! A large Angelic Chariot swooped overhead and a variety of animals flitted past on the trails. Standing under a large, perfectly shaped elm tree were three figures waving gently in their direction – a giant brown Kodiak, a smaller polar and a tiny meerkat. Family!

Magda halted the flitting procession and advanced to the three animal spirits who stood smiling at her and her charges. "God's blessings on you all."

"And on you!" came the returning chorus.

"Gentle spirits. May I present your living mortal relatives from Earth Alpha. Bearoness Belinda Béarnaise Bruin Bear (nee Black); Her spouse, the celebrated genius, Doctor Octavius Bear and their associate, Mr. Mauritius Meerkat. You, of course, know me and Director Raymond but you may or may not know one of heaven's more famous recent citizens, Lady Juliet Armstrong, the former Baroness Crestwell and her canine companion, Pookie."

She turned to the Octavians. "And now, let me introduce your relatives. Bearoness, this lovely polar sow is Beartha Black. your mother." Belinda growled and rushed to embrace her. Hugs as only bears can hug. Even when one is evanescent.

"Doctor Bear, perhaps you recognize this elegant ursine boar as your father, Jupiter Bear." Somewhat restrained, the two Kodiak giants bowed to each other and then grasped paws.

"And finally, Mr. Meerkat, this vivacious young lady is your sister Mabel." The saucy suricate squeaked and threw herself at Maury. He jumped back but then wrapped his tail around his diminutive sibling.

Magda smiled and said, "Director Raymond, Lady Juliet, Pookie, Orifiel and I will move away for a short time and allow you all to become reacquainted without any interference on our part. I hope, Mr. Meerkat, you will come away convinced of Heaven's reality and absence of trickery. We need Octavian assistance." The invisible guardian angels who had accompanied the travelers also withdrew.

*****

The family members separated and took up seats on luxurious benches along one of the golden paths. Each pair somewhat clumsily re-established relations.

Jupiter put his paw on Octavius' arm and said, "Well, Son. You seem to have done quite well for yourself. Even here in Paradise, your reputation precedes you. A fabulous tycoon, a formidable polymath and famous criminologist par excellence all in one. To say nothing of your magnificent wife and two exceptional juveniles. How is your mother? I am still quite fond of Juno. She was my favorite wife. Beautiful, smart and oh, so feisty."

"She is quite well, Dad. She has a comfortable den on Kodiak Island. Refuses to live with me in Ohio. As you know she is a staunch traditionalist. I speak to her often and provide for her and Florence, her Arctic Fox maid. Belinda and I have been leading quite interesting and exciting lives along with our twins and our associates, the Octavians."

"Ah yes, the Octavians. That meerkat fellow seems to be something of a 'Doubting Thomas' when it comes to Heaven and the Queen's mission."

"Maury sees his major function as keeping Belinda, the Twins and me out of harm's way. He'll come around. Do you know what this mysterious mission is all about?"

"No. We were just asked to meet you and prove Paradise really exists. I hope we're succeeding."

"As far as I'm concerned, you are. Are you enjoying your joyful afterlife in Paradise?"

"Joy is exactly the right word, Son. Heaven is not so much a place as a state of being and joyfulness describes it best. I hope you and yours will be blessed in a similar fashion when your life on Earth Alpha ends."

"Thank you, Dad. I hope you're right. I wonder how Belinda and Beartha are doing."

On a similar bench further along the golden path, the two Polar sows were enthusiastically recollecting their personal histories. Beartha recalled her accident on the Alaska ice floe and Belinda remembered how her aunt Donna stepped in and took care of the cub prodigy. She told her about her career as a prima aqueuse with the Aquabears and of course, her on-again, off-again romances with Octavius. Both bears sighed ecstatically about Beartha's irrepressible genius grandchildren, Arabella and McTavish.

"You've been leading a charmed and blessed life, Belinda, or should I say, milady. A daughter of mine as a fabulous Scottish Bearoness. Imagine!

"Mom, do you recall a twin brother of mine, Barton?"

"Yes, but I died not too soon after his birth. Did Donna take him in as well?"

"She did but as soon as he reached post juvenile stage, he disappeared. He only reappeared last month at my resort/palace, Polar Paradise. Looking for a job. Octavius hired him as a computer specialist."

"Oh, computers! I'm so glad we don't need them here in Heaven. Well. I'm happy you two got reunited. It's gone well?"

"Yes, but another reunion turned out to be a disaster. An Alaskan Senator, Polonius Polar, claimed he was a Black and my father, wedded to you. We used modern DNA technology to prove he was a fraud but not before he murdered his assistant who was blackmailing him. He'll be standing trial shortly in Scotland. Octavius and I will be witnesses." *(See Book 20. The Case of the Polar Politician)*

"Oh, dear, how terrible. I don't ever remember a Polonius or an Alaskan Senator. Your father, Porter, was an ordinary Polar Boar who made a living fishing along with his mates. He left soon after you two were born. Not unusual. I hope this Polonius character gets his comeuppance."

"I'm sure he will. Earth Alpha Scottish Justice is pretty stringent. American Senator or not."

"Well, I'm sure our little visit will be coming to an end shortly. This Mary Magdalen and Director Raymond seem to have things under control along with the guardian angels. Do you know this other Baroness? Juliet Armstrong, is it?"

"We just met her. She seems to be our heavenly liaison. Queen Mary, with the permission of the Almighty, wants to send Octavius, the Octavians and me on a cosmic undertaking of some sort. It's also supposed to involve Sherlock Holmes from Earth Beta."

"Oooh, I've heard of him. He's a great detective like Octavius. But tell me. I've really enjoyed this get together but why are you here.?

"Because Octavius' associate, Maury Meerkat, thinks this is all a scam. This is to prove that Heaven and it's denizens are real. Director Raymond and Mary Magdalen are seeing to it. I think his sister, Mabel is convincing him."

*****

"So, you're the executive assistant to that giant Kodiak. I understand he and his wife are worth gazillions. Are you rich?"

"Yes and No. I lead a very comfortable life on the whole. Octavius did me a great favor by saving me from a Mauritian jail. We've had some very, let me say, interesting adventures. This is one of them. I'm also a very successful theatrical agent. Some of my biggest clients are Octavians. A star singer and actress; a magic Tarot act; a rock band and even the Bearoness herself. She's a lead aqueuse with the Aquabears swimming troupe. Although nowadays she's mostly retired from the pool and diving board and is concentrating on running her resort and cruise businesses. They're growing like gangbusters. Speaking of gangs, Mabel. What happened to our old mob?"

"Most of them are dead, Maury. Mom and Dad are here. So is Monty. I can call them up for you, if you want. The rest of them are still in Purgatory. I hope they get out soon. Except for Max. He's in hell. Too much of an offender, I'm afraid."

"I'd like to see Mom and Dad. Monty and I never got along. He said I was a snotty kid."

Mabel laughed, "Well, you were, you know. A real smart Alec. OK, let me get the folks." She looked skyward, murmured something Maury couldn't hear and clapped her forepaws. After several moments two figures were seen flitting across a green field toward the pair.

"Here they come." A small female meerkat squeaked, "Morey, darling. Is it really you? Did you die? When? How? Oh, it's so good to see your pointy little nose, isn't it Dad?"

The somewhat larger male nodded and extended his paw to the very much alive Mauritius. *(Not his real name. He was named Morey at birth and changed it when he was captured playing lookout for a mob of meerkat jewel thieves on the Indian Ocean island. Octavius took him in paw and his conversion is history.)*

"Hello Son, Welcome to Paradise. But you don't look supernatural. Does he, Martha? Mabel?

His sister laughed. "No, Dad, Mom, he's not dead, at least not yet. *(squeaky giggles)* Are you, Morey or Maury?"

"No, I'm still alive although looking around here and at you all, dying doesn't seem to be a bad idea. Of course, I'd have to be admitted to Paradise. I hope I've been sufficiently penitent and upright to earn entrance. We'll see."

His mother, as curious as all members of her species, screeched. "It's wonderful to see you but why are you here?"

"I'm part of a team being commissioned by the Queen of Heaven to prevent major disasters on Earths Alpha and Beta."

"Wow, but what does that have to do with us?"

"Er, well, you see. Up until an hour or so ago, I didn't believe in Heaven. I thought it was some kind of scam. Call it a meerkat's suspicious nature. But seeing you three and your surroundings, I guess I'll have to admit Paradise is real. Are you all happy?"

"Happy doesn't describe it. This isn't just a place. It's a condition. Unlimited joy. Whatever this mission is, you should be eager to carry it out. The Queen and her entourage are all wonderful. If she wants something, it must truly be grand!"

At that point, Magda appeared and greeted the Meerkat. Orifiel, unseen, stood by. "Mauritius, It's time to rejoin the Bearoness, Pookie and Doctor Bear back at the Celestial Executive Complex. They're waiting for you. If you are convinced that Heaven exists, we have an important job for your team. We need to plan and make assignments. Let's flit back."

Maury bade his tearful mother and sister good-bye and shook paws with his father. Off they flitted.

Over the scenic gardens and park to the Elysian Fields and sparkling administrative towers. Juliet, Pookie and Director Raymond were nowhere to be found.

Magda looked at Maury. "Are you persuaded and ready to assist in this project?"

"Yes, I guess so but what is it?"

"Lady Juliet and her dog will be along shortly and you can all return to your mansion on Earth Alpha – the Bear's Lair, is it? Clever name. She will outline what is required. One more thing. When you return to Earth Alpha, you will all have forgotten you have made this journey to Paradise. You'll be willing and prepared to work with the Baroness who will be coordinating your activities. It's been a pleasure being with you and on behalf of Mary, Queen of Heaven and the Almighty, thank you and God's blessings on you." She disappeared.

*****

While the three Octavians were renewing family ties, Director Raymond had approached the Baroness, "Lady Juliet, since you've been chosen to act as liaison for this project with both the Octavians and Sherlock Holmes, I'd better bring you up to speed on the situation. Mother Mary does not engage living mortals in such projects lightly or often. Will you and Pookie join me in some ambrosia and nectar and we'll discuss the circumstances? Then after you are well informed, we can include Doctor Bear, Bearoness Belinda and the Meerkat. I believe by now, his doubts about Paradise have been dealt with. We'll see when Magdalen returns with them."

They took up a bench. Pookie sat demolishing a Heavenly Chewy with one eye fixed on Juliet. The Baroness stared at Director Raymond who was silent for the moment. "Raymond, as I understand it: The Queen has discovered a massive plot by Professor Moriarty and this horse, General Turmoil to reduce Earth Alpha and Beta to slave colonies. I suppose it involves killing off or taking over most of those worlds' governments, institutions, infrastructure, commerce, military and influential populations and establishing control with chosen traitors and quislings. Then they propose to extend their control to other exoplanets in the Cosmos. Madness!"

"Correct, Baroness. The Queen, with the guidance of the Almighty, wants you to coordinate a campaign led by Sherlock Holmes and Octavius Bear to thwart their plans and ambitions."

"Why did she choose me? I have very little experience counteracting plots and cabals. Even with Holmes and Watson."

"But Holmes and Watson do and you are their colleague. Octavius Bear and his troupe have prevented wars and have taken on General Turmoil several times. First persuade him and his team to deal with this crazy Horse and then you can talk Holmes and Watson into going after Moriarty once again."

"So I am to be Persuader in Chief?"

"If that's how you want to look at it, then yes."

"Well, I suppose the first thing we need to do, now that the Meerkat seems convinced is to get them back to the Bear's Lair and wipe their memories. How do I explain my role?"

"Just tell the truth. The things we don't want them to remember are they visited Heaven, met Queen Mary, Magda and me and saw their families. You can tell them about your affiliation with Holmes and the Queen's mission. They won't know exactly why, but they'll believe you. Don't enlighten them any further."

"All right! Pookie and I will handle it. Let's get them back to Earth Alpha. I think Maury is relieved of his doubts. We shall see.

Chapter Five

Belinda, Octavius and Maury stood in the Bearoness' suite. They felt as if they had passed through a slight tremor in time. No memory of their recent celestial trip.

Pause, rewind and repeat!

Belinda giggled, "Surprise! Doctor Octavius Bear, let me introduce Lady Juliet Armstrong, Baroness Crestwell formerly of the Earth Beta United Kingdom, lately of the Heavenly Kingdom of Paradise. She and her little dog Pookie, are spirits. They are here on a mission from the Almighty. They want our help. Funny, it's usually the other way around."

"Oh God!" exclaimed Octavius and then sputtered at what he had just said. "Forgive me, Baroness. I've never thought of the Omnipotent as clients. What could I possibly do for them?"

The meerkat simply gaped. No recollection of recent events.

Pookie recognized the need for momentary distraction. She skipped over to Maury. They were both about the same size. She flirted, nuzzled him and hopped away, returned and danced on her hind legs and then her forepaws. She repeated the exercise. Finally she executed her signature backflip.

In spite of himself, the theatrical agent meerkat laughed. "Dog, No matter where you're from or who you are, we have to get you together with Madame Giselle and Otto. You'd be a sensational addition to their act."

Juliet smiled. "Her name is Pookie and she's already something of a show business sensation. She dances and she's a star member of the True Angels Aerobatic Team and three time winner of their Top Dogfighting Award. She's a very accomplished flyer. Unfortunately, she can't talk and her normal state is incorporeal. In short, she's a ghost as am I. I'm here as an emissary from the Queen of Heaven. We'd like you to take on a critical mission to preserve your world and what was once mine."

Belinda and Octavius stared at her. The Great Bear snorted. "I'm fascinated and puzzled. Who and what is this threat and why me? I assume you'll want my colleagues."

"The Octavians? Oh yes! Why you? You've dealt with this kind of menace in the past. I assume you are familiar with a sociopathic horse called General Turmoil. He is off on a campaign to subdue and destroy most of two worlds leaving only a small number of slaves to maintain the infrastructure. He then plans to use the remnants of Earths Alpha and Beta as jumping off points for conquering the entire Cosmos. Heaven seldom intervenes but this situation is most grave and must be dealt with speedily and effectively."

Octavius winced. "So, Turmoil's gone over the edge. He's insane. Who are his supporters?"

"Mostly rogue members of his organization. You know it as The Business. However, there is more. It's why I'm involved. Turmoil is joined by Professor James Moriarty. Pookie and I have teamed with Sherlock Holmes in a terrestrial/celestial partnership. It was he who brought my killers to justice."

Maury gaped. "Sherlock Holmes? So he's real and you were killed?"

"Yes, a tale for another time. Holmes is very real. He has been a long-time opponent of General Turmoil's partner, Moriarty. We need to stop him, too. However, our first task is to deal with the Horse. He's supplying the technology and armaments and enabling the professor to Quantum and Time Travel between the two worlds. Millions of light years separate the two and Earth Alpha is over a hundred thirty years ahead in development. The General is up for that but then, so are you and your team."

"After that, our next step is to convince Holmes that Moriarty's still alive and persuade him to join us in cutting the Professor down. Are you willing to participate and do you want to involve your Octavians?"

"The Great Bear looked at Belinda and Maury. Both nodded their head in agreement."

"OK, Maury. Let's gather the clan!"

Juliet grinned. A thought crossed her mind. She needed to make Holmes aware of these near miraculous devices she'd heard of. Ursula? They could be so very valuable to him. Let's see what they will tell her.

She peered at Octavius. "Before you do that, can you tell me about this Deep Data Lab you have over in Kentucky. It's called the Hexagon, isn't it? Is that where those amazing Ursulas come from?"

"Yes it is. We try to keep them secret but in your case, you have a need to know. Just a moment and I'll call up L.Condor, the Chief Technical Officer of the Advanced Super Computing Center at the Deep Data Hexagon." A screen came to life showing a large Andean Condor at a desk with a cluster of screens surrounding him. A Bonobo was sitting on one of the chairs in front of the desk.

The chimpanzee looked up at a screen "Hello. Doctor Bear. You're back from Australia?"

"Hello, Byzantia, yes I am. Finished another round of crime fighting. Can I get your boss' attention?"

The condor took his eyes away from the screens he had been watching and acknowledged the Bear's presence. "Octavius, Good to see you back. What can we do for you?"

"I want to introduce you to someone quite unusual. Actually, two someones." Juliet appeared on the screen next to him. She had the dog in her arms. "Baroness, let me present Mr. L. Condor, Chief Technical Officer (CTO) of the Advanced Super Computing Center-Deep Data Hexagon and his highly talented assistant, Byzantia Bonobo. She is responsible for the Ursula program."

"Byzz and Condo, say hello to Lady Juliet Armstrong, Baroness Crestwell and her very clever canine associate Ms. Pookie. They are both ghosts."

Byzz' jaw dropped and Condo laughed. "Well, Octavius. Your trip to Australia sharpened your sense of humor. Who are they, really?"

Juliet intervened. "No joke, Senhor Condor, Pookie and I are here at Heaven's command to take on your world's General Turmoil and an Earth Beta fiend named Professor Moriarty. They have plans to conquer the Universe.

Doctor Bear has agreed to help us. Pookie and I are indeed spirits, formerly from Earth Beta, both deceased but highly active."

Octavius said, "I'll be calling the Octavians together shortly to outline plans for dealing with them. We'll be calling on Sherlock Holmes on Earth Beta to work with us."

Byzz reacted. "There is a Sherlock Holmes? I thought he was a fiction."

Octavius laughed. 'He probably will think we and all of Earth Alpha are fictional. But first, the Baroness has expressed deep interest in the Hexagon and especially the Ursulas. Given her celestial status, I think we can safely reveal some of our secrets to her. If you can't trust Heaven, who can you trust?"

Condo was a bit dubious but decided to comply. "With all due modesty, Baroness. the Advanced Super Computing Center at the Deep Data Hexagon is the most cutting edge technology entity on Earth Alpha, perhaps even the entire universe. There are several government and private sector institutions that approach our sophistication. That includes General Turmoil's group called The Business. But between Howard Watt's Multiverse Project and our computing and telecommunications capabilities, UUI leads. From the Twins' electronic games to our sophisticated satellite systems, our AI developments, our malware suppression techniques and software, firmware, hardware products, the Hexagon is a hot bed of technology leadership. Our scientists and engineers are of the very finest. Speaking of whom, let me allow Byzz to tell you more about our pride and joy, the highly secret but quite amazing Ursula program,"

Byzz smiled and said, "Rather than me prattling on about the project, let me introduce our most recent model, Ursula 17. We have several newer versions under development but she is our current workhorse." She pressed a few keys on her console and a lynx appeared on the screens. "Here is that highly essential and near-miraculous member of the Octavians – Ursula – Universal Ursine Intellect Model 17 – Artificial General Intelligence System (AGI). I'll let her explain herself."

The lynx image smiled and winked. "Hello Baroness! Hello, little Pookie! My official nomenclature is Universal Ursine Intellect Model 17– Artificial General Intelligence System (AGI). Ursula 17 for short. My predecessor systems and I were developed by the Advanced Super Computing Center of UUI. I am the result of the Computing Center team using those earlier versions to create a further enhanced entity – me, the Model 17, which, we are sure, will help produce even more sophisticated, independent and powerful AGI systems in the near future. Each advanced unit maintains the capabilities, memories and power of its progenitors so in a sense, we are not replacing but rather expanding the Ursula family. Ursula 18 is under extensive development and field trials."

"While I am physically supported by a highly secure and hyper-powered server farm at the Kentucky Hexagon, I also exist independently in clouds and network-based nodes and can be simultaneously incorporated into a wide variety of separate devices like this laptop unit. I combine quantum computing elements with extremely high speed conventional circuits. I have practically limitless data capacity and 6G+ transmission speed. My super high-velocity multi-tasking abilities and algorithms allow me to continuously serve an exceptionally large number of entities while simultaneously and autonomously enhancing my own capabilities. In short. I'm powerful and fast."

"Depending on the physical unit in which I'm housed, I can see, hear, feel and smell. I speak and understand an almost infinite number of languages and dialects. I can change my appearance and my vocal output to suit most moods and situations. Ursula 18 will be equipped with even more Quantum, Virtual and Augmented Reality functions than I already have. I can interact with other devices, vehicles and structures and of course, all varieties of sentient animals in this world and others."

"I am also an important component of the Multiverse Project and I adapt my capabilities to deal with alternate universes as they are discovered."

"I have restraining functions which prevent me from doing deliberate harm even in self-defense, unless I am released by a recognized authority using very carefully protected clandestine codes. Finally, I have been told that although the Ursulas are shy on emotions, I have developed a finely-honed sense of humor. I need it in this job. LOL!"

Juliet, who understood approximately 20% of what she had heard, looked confused. "LOL?"

They all chuckled. Octavius said, "It's Internet slang, It means laughing out loud. I realize you heavenly denizens have no need for technology but your exposure to Earth Alpha will certainly add to your experiences and vocabulary. Thanks, Condo and Byzz. I'm gathering the clan to discuss this situation. Both of you join us. Given the topic is the General, your input is essential. It'll take a few minutes for the group to assemble. See you on the screens."

Juliet was amazed. "Thank you, Octavius. That was fabulous. I'm sure our Angelic Communications teams are up on all of this but I definitely am not." She thought. Holmes needed to know about the Earth Alpha tech capabilities. I wonder if he will understand it. I certainly don't. Do you, Pookie?

The dog whined.

Octavius chortled, "Oh, Baroness. We may be ahead of the rest of the technological world but what I would give to have your celestial capabilities.'

The Baroness grinned, "One of these days, Octavius. One of these days! You'll love it."

They left the suite and headed for the elevators down to the conference rooms. Juliet and Pookie remained corporeal. Orifiel was his/her evanescent self

*****

Several large and fully equipped conference rooms took up the entirety of one of the mansion's sublevels. Calls went out on cell phones and Ursulas to summon the team for an all-hands meeting . The unadorned white walls of the room were solid and soundproof. On a modest stage, an elevating podium that could rise to Octavius' nine foot height or lower to Maury's diminutive size was set at full altitude. Clearly, the Great Bear was in charge of the meeting. Chairs were already set up conference style. Condo, Byzz and Marlin were on the Zoom screens as were several of the Polar Paradise staff in the Shetlands. As the local Octavians arrived, they took up seats appropriate to their height, girth and shape. Coffee, tea and soft drinks were laid out on a sideboard. The usual chatter was intermixed with sounds of clinking bowls and moving chairs. An invisible cluster of Guardian Angels hovered about. Octavius, Belinda and Maury entered. The Bearoness and Meerkat took up seats in front while the Great Bear strode to the podium and stood at full height. Unseen, Baroness Juliet, Pookie and Orifiel stood in the back. She was ready to appear on Octavius' cue.

The Bear looked over the room and spoke to a strategically placed Ursula. "Is everybody here?" The unit chimed and replied. "All Octavians present and accounted for."

He cleared his throat, a sound equivalent to a Category Five Hurricane. Octavius never needed a microphone or amplification. In fact, he was lethal over the telephone. Listeners had to hold the instrument far away from their ears and then move it close up in order to reply. More often they just used speakerphone mode.

For all of his skills, the Great Bear was a lousy public speaker. He knew it but still insisted on accepting most invitations he received. Behind his massive back, he was known as the Boring Bear. His current audience accepted it. After all, he's the Boss.

He began with that time-worn chestnut. "I suppose you're wondering why I summoned you all here?"

This induced a series of snorts, chirps, barks and chuckles. He went on. "We have received an assignment from the Very Highest Authority and Belinda and I have decided to accept it. After you have heard the details, you each have the option to participate or not as you see fit. We will make a similar proposition to the staff at Polar Paradise. Lucky for you, I do not plan to speak much longer. Our next guest will tell you all about this commission which has my full approval."

He turned to an empty space on the stage to the right of the podium and nodded. Out of nowhere, a beautiful, dark haired woman in a fashionable scarlet gown popped into view. She was smiling and holding a Bichon Frisé in her arms who looked for all the world like Madame Giselle. Members of the audience stared at the woman and back and forth between the two dogs. Giselle was wearing her gold lamé turban. This one was wearing a red bow and a halo, slightly askew. The woman's halo was tilted rakishly over her left ear.

Shock at their appearance and then an undertow of comments, stares and questions.

Octavius chuckled. "Your reaction is the same as mine. Let me introduce Lady Juliet Armstrong Baroness Crestwell, originally from London on Earth Beta but now deceased and an emissary from Mary, the Queen of Heaven."

The Twins - Arabella and McTavish - immediately got going with an Ursula, recording all of this for inclusion in one of their upcoming electronic games.

Chita, as usual, reacted first. "Oh, Tavi. You are too much. You honestly expect us to believe these two are ghosts sent here to give us a heavenly assignment? Come on! Very neat theatrics. You should hire them, Maury."

Juliet laughed in her posh contralto, "You don't know how close to the truth you are, Ms. Chita. In my mortal days, I was the star of many London

West End musicals. Bearoness Belinda and I have already shared our show business reminiscences. You're a singer currently from London as well as other venues. We'll have to compare the Earth Alpha and Beta versions of the city. But difficult as it may be for all of you to accept, Pookie and I – she stroked the dog – are now truly denizens of Paradise. I am here because I have had dealings in the past with mortals on Earth Beta, specifically Sherlock Holmes. This is my first venture on Earth Alpha. You folks are far ahead of my original world in technological, social, medical, scientific and educational matters but we still both suffer from a substantial dose of evil and criminal behavior. Satan has cosmic reach. Dealing with it is your profession. I am here to ask you to apply your talents to topple the plans of conquest of General Turmoil, your old foe and his villainous Earth Beta partner, Professor Moriarty."

At the mention of the equine criminal, the group stirred and murmured to each other.

Juliet let them settle down, and said, "Let me explain further. Heaven seldom intervenes in the affairs of mortals. Of course, each one of us is blessed with a Guardian Angel and our prayers are received and accepted in Paradise on a constant basis. But the Almighty created us all with free wills and it is up to us to conduct our lives accordingly. However, every now and again, a situation arises that requires celestial involvement. This is one of them and I have been sent to invoke your assistance. It entails the planned defeat and near total destruction of the civilizations of Earth Beta and here on Earth Alpha. If General Turmoil and his partner in crime, Professor James Moriarty succeed, only a force of mindless mercenaries will be left in either world poised to attack the rest of the Cosmos."

More murmuring and rumbling. Frau Schuylkill, the beautiful she-wolf, looked at Juliet. "That's a horrible prospect but surely Heaven can deal with it. Some well-placed lightning bolts or an assault by an army of angels. Just kill the felons off."

"God has decided that mortals must defend their own existence. Mary, the Queen of Heaven has been given the mandate to put a plan in motion to support you and I am her agent."

The she-wolf's companion, Colonel Wyatt Where growled and said, "Fine, but we have armies to deal with this kind of stuff. Why do you need us?"

"Because you have the unique scientific expertise to thwart their efforts. They have taken over an unpopulated but livable exoplanet as a staging area for their assaults. They have already built up a stockpile of sophisticated weapons and support technology in preparation for their invasions."

"Good, let's just blow the damn place up."

"The Queen has specified that no lives are to be lost, even the criminals."

The wolf was nonplussed. "Your Queen…

"Our Queen!"

"OK, Our Queen isn't making it very easy, is she?"

"Lives are precious and they must be spared if possible."

Howard Watt, the Quantum Travel genius porcupine was taking all of this in. He turned to the screen showing L.Condor, the Chief Technical Officer of the Advanced Super Computing Center. "Condo, I think we have the means to deal with this. We've done it before. Remember those crazy Birds?"

"Yes. It was amazing how all their weaponry and technology suddenly disappeared. Swallowed up by their star, wasn't it? Can we do it again?"

"Don't see why not! We're going to need a few Ursulas to carry it off. You can help, Colonel. To do a weapons analysis. Do you have the location of this exoplanet, Baroness?"

She nodded and held up a piece of celestial paper. Director Raymond had thought of everything. "It's called Planet W."

Otto had been sitting next to his Tarot partner, Giselle. He looked at Juliet and piped up. "Wait a second. I'm dubious like Chita. Octavius, Belinda, Maury! You believe all this? We only have this so-called ghost's say-so that this staging planet exists and this whole conquest cabal is real.'

The Great Bear knew he believed and trusted the Baroness although he couldn't exactly say why. Belinda grinned and nodded. Maury shrugged but agreed. The heavenly memory wipe was working.

Juliet smiled at the otter. "You're Sir Otto the Magnificent, aren't you. I'm delighted to meet you. In a little while, could I interest you in a trip to Earth Beta? I'm going to need an assist with Sherlock Holmes in dealing with Moriarty. He thinks the professor is dead. I'd like you and Doctor Bear to convince him otherwise but first we have to deal with the General's chicanery. Doctor Howard! Can you really make all their war materiel just disappear?"

"I believe we can without most of us even leaving the Bear's Lair. I'll have to speak further with Condo and Marlin. I think we'll need an Ursula or two and Colonel Wyatt Where to do a reconnaissance." Marlin is a dolphin scientist and Howard Watt's Multiverse Program partner. He was participating in the discussion by closed circuit TV from his sizeable tank in the Quantum Travel lab one level down. He smacked his massive flippers and agreed. "Baroness, when it comes to remote transit, the General is good but we're much better. We can clean him out, several times if necessary."

Octavius stood up. "OK. Let's get started. Those cosmic conquerors are not going to wait on us. Baroness Juliet, do have anything else? If not, we can regroup in the Quantum Lab."

"No, just to say, 'God's blessings on all of you. Sir Otto, can we get together a bit later?"

She had let Pookie down on the floor. The Bichon jumped from the stage and scampered over to Giselle and Otto. The two Bichons sniffed and barked at each other. Then Pookie stood on her hind legs, pranced and did a triple backflip. Not to be outdone, Otto with his acrobatic gifts, replied with his own shuffling caper. The two ended with synchronized somersaults to the laughter and delight of the assemblage. Giselle clapped her paws.

Howard and Wyatt went down to join Marlin in the Quantum Travel lab and begin their own cycle of destruction. Condo joined them on the screens.

71

Juliet and Pookie followed with the invisible Orifiel, staring in wonderment at the devices, gauges, dashboards and equipment that lined the walls of the sterile space. Marlin was splashing about in his residential tank. At one end was an impressive console, no doubt waterproof and shaped to accommodate his facile flippers. It matched another console set on one wall. He greeted the ghosts who bowed back at him. A large ovoid ring occupied the center of the room with a thick, wide pad sitting on each side of it. The dog proceeded on a sniffing fact finding mission, squeezing under tables and stands and jumping back and forth through the ring.

The porcupine smiled at the Baroness. "Welcome to the Octavian Multiverse Travel Lab. This is where we launch our Quantum voyages to other worlds and exoplanets. Colonel Where and an Ursula system will be leaving shortly to size up the situation on exoplanet W. We've checked the coordinates you've provided and they are spot on."

The Baroness grinned, "Of course. They were supplied by Angelic Transport. They never miss a destination."

Howard chuckled, "I wish we were that accurate. Please get Pookie out of the ring. If we accidentally hit a switch or two she may go soaring off into the unknown. Or maybe not, since she's an amorphous spirit."

Juliet laughed, "Let's not find out. Pookie, come here, sweetheart. Of course, we can flit and transit throughout the Cosmos on our own celestial power. When the Colonel and his Ursula companion fly off, we'd like to go with them."

"Of course. By the way, you call it flitting. We call it zapping. The Colonel and Otto are our most experienced zappers although I have made a good number of trips."

Wyatt came over to the three of them. "Hello again, Baroness Crestwell. Do I understand you'll be coming with Ursula and me on our recce mission?"

"If that's not a problem, Colonel. I need to report back to Heaven on the nature of the General's fiendish plot and resources."

"No problem at all. I'll be happy to describe what he's got and what he can do. I hope he doesn't have the Doomsday Weapon."

"Doomsday Weapon??"

"A nuclear cobalt bomb whose explosive power is limited, leaving most of the target's infrastructure intact but whose radiation is intense enough to kill off all life forms who are not shielded. The radiation dies off quickly after creating its fatal carnage leaving, forgive me, a ghost world fit to be re-inhabited by the aggressors' minions. It would ideally fit their intentions of taking over Earth Alpha and Beta as launch sites for Cosmic invasions."

Juliet blanched, "Oh, how horrible. Howard, can you really dispose of those weapons if they are there?"

"Yes, Baroness. Exoplanet W orbits a Red Dwarf star more than hot enough to destroy anything or anybody propelled onto its surface."

"My mandate is to avoid deliberately killing anyone even if they are evil incarnate. Heavenly orders. I don't suppose we can avoid accidents. Where is the General?"

"His offices are in Washington DC but at the moment he may be anywhere."

"Well then, Colonel, any time you and Ursula are ready so are Pookie and I. *(Orifiel would be coming with them.)*

The door to the Lab opened and the beautiful she-wolf padded in. "Just wanted to see my adventurous mate off on his journey. I'm not enthused about Quantum Travel but he seems to enjoy it."

Wyatt patted her paw. "Don't worry, Ilse. We'll be back in a twinkling."

"Ach, see that you are! I can't fly the Twin Otter by myself and we have to get Otto and Giselle up to New York for their TV show."

They both laughed. "Always the true sentimentalist, my dear. OK, Howard. I have my oxygen mask tested and on standby. Ready when you are. Ursula. Are you onboard?"

The lynx image on the AGI's laptop winked and a chime rang out.

Wyatt laid down in the transport ring, extending a paw to the Baroness who in turn was holding Pookie tight. The two of them went incorporeal. The Ursula was strapped around Wyatt's shoulder. Orifiel folded his wings and stepped into the space.

Howard looked up at Marlin. "Are we synchronized?"

"Locked in and ready." They simultaneously flipped several switches and a brief whine echoed though the room followed by a rushing whoosh. The travelers had disappeared."

Howard, Marlin and Ilse looked up at large screen displaying galaxies, stars and planets. A small shape rushed through the darkened space, eventually slowed and stopped on a barely hospitable oversized planetoid orbiting a Red Dwarf star. They had arrived on Exoplanet W.

They circled the exoplanet looking for buildings and signs of life. Several areas looked likely. They'd have to get nearer to find out what was really down there. It had been fairly routine thus far. Now came the interesting part. It was up to the Colonel to interpret what they saw. The Baroness knew practically nothing about weaponry. They expected arms and other war matériel. But what kinds? Enough to wipe out a world? How many soldiers were there and who were they? Time for a closer look

Down they went. Lady Juliet, Pookie and Orifiel gently flitted toward the barren ground. Not so Wyatt.

Chapter Six

Thump! "Damn! Landing is always the toughest. Hey Baroness! Are you and your dog OK?"

Juliet and Pookie rematerialized. "We're fine, Colonel. Incorporeal flitting is standard procedure for us. Are you alright? Did Ursula make it?" She looked for Orifiel who was shaking out his furled wings.

"I'm fine. Just getting a little old for these planetary crash landings. Howard and Marlin are working on softening the touchdowns but it's still a bit rough. I wonder how far we are from the General's lethal stash. Any idea, Ursula?"

"About a mile away, Colonel. We passed over several buildings. I'll check again." Ursula rang her chime and began communicating back to the Quantum Lab. It would take a while to report even at the speed of light.

Juliet picked up another Ursula and whispered to the Colonel, "Let Pookie and I go scouting, invisibly of course. When we find the weapons, we can return the compliment and fly you over so you can evaluate what we've uncovered. Meanwhile, stay hidden. They most certainly have surveillance devices and patrols to protect their caches. They won't detect Pookie, Orifiel or me."

Ursula gave her directions and she and the dog flitted off accompanied by the AGI and ever present but always invisible Orifiel.

Wyatt was impressed at how clever and gutsy this British noblewoman was. Certainly not a bit of brainless fluff he had been led to believe they all were. An actress and Sherlock Holmes' colleague to boot. Commissioned by the Queen of Heaven. Quite a package!

In the middle of nowhere stood several gigantic warehouses carefully enclosed by barbed wire and surrounded by several guard posts. Flood lights illuminated the entire area and a patrol of horses walked the perimeter. Large roll-up doors seemed to be the only entry into the vast buildings. Outside the fence, a huge number of aircraft and armored transports sat, guns pointed ominously forward. The General had certainly managed his logistics quite efficiently, procuring and transporting supplies for a major assault. The tank-like combat vehicles were large enough to accommodate several horses but were probably destined for use by the subservient survivors on both Earths after the systematic slaughter of the primary populations.

Juliet and Pookie flitted through the door of the largest warehouse and found themselves facing a gigantic horde of weaponry and technological devices. The instruments of destruction. She whispered to her Ursula. "Get the Colonel on the line."

"Wyatt, stay there. This place is heavily guarded. You'd be picked up in an instant. Ursula is sending you photos of the materiel stored here in the warehouse. I'm sure this is a weapons depot and needs to be destroyed but see if you can pick out those so-called Doomsday bombs. That will tell us how dastardly their plans are. Utter annihilation! No wonder Heaven was so concerned."

The Colonel took a moment to scan the incoming images and growled. "Yes, there they are. That's why they have the place so carefully guarded. I'm going to move. They can probably pick up the transmissions between the Ursulas and will go looking for the source. They won't understand the encrypted messaging but they'll know someone is transmitting. Stay invisible and get the Hell out of there. *(Sorry!)* Can you circle the rest of the exoplanet and see if there are any more of these depots? I'm sending the coordinates of this one back to Howard. When we know how many there are, he and Marlin can send them all on a one way trip to the star."

The Baroness signed off. She, Pookie and Orifiel took off in three different directions and flitted at high speed around the periphery of the exoplanet. They found two more identical warehouses and one building that looked like a command center and housing for equine personnel. Respecting the Queen's instructions, she was reluctant to kill off the occupants even if they were prospective murderers. She needed to get them out of the building before it went plummeting into oblivion. She sent the coordinates back and sped through the building looking for a fire alarm. She spotted one, materialized and pulled it. Sirens and klaxons bawled as she returned to her evanescent state and a group of horses raced for the exits. One or two stayed behind to deal with the nonexistent fire but at least she tried to get them all out.

Several minutes passed and suddenly the first warehouse ripped away from its foundations and flew into space with all of its deadly contents heading for a collision with the red dwarf. The tank-like vehicles and aircraft accompanied it. Another moment and two more buildings flew overhead on a similar voyage. Finally, the command center, fire alarms still blaring, headed over the horizon out into space and onward to the star. The horses stood dumbstruck and shivering with fear. The commander neighed and tried to pull his troops together. He called the General's headquarters on Earth Alpha and described what had happened.

General Turmoil immediately realized who was behind this. Octavius Bear! Only he had the ability to wreak that kind of destruction. He decided reluctantly to abandon the exoplanet and regroup. A temporary setback. He would deal with the Bear and resume his plans. He needed to confer with Moriarty.

*****

Meanwhile Juliet, Pookie, the Colonel, Orifiel and the two Ursulas were being transported back to the Multiverse Lab at the Bear's Lair.

The Baroness. Pookie and Orifiel arrived in non-material form and landed gracefully on the pads on the Lab floor. The Colonel wasn't so lucky and painfully hit the mat with a resounding thud. He caught his breath and looked over at Howard. "When are you guys going to adjust that landing speed. We fly back and forth across the universe safely but damn near break our necks on touchdown back here at the Lair. The Baroness and her dog came in safely because they're not substantial. And no, I don't plan to die in order to flit. Maybe Ilse will decide to kill me off."

The she-wolf had been standing by and awaiting his arrival. Laughing, she extended her paws and helped him to his feet. Juliet and Pookie re-materialized. Octavius and Howard patted the Colonel on the back. "Good job. Those weapon are all demolished."

"Congratulate the Baroness and her dog. They did all the work."

*****

Back in the Bear's Lair Lounge, the Octavians, bowls of liquid spirits in paw, were listening to the Colonel, Juliet. Howard, and the Ursulas tell their tale (tail?) of weapons destruction. Marlin was paying attention from his tank and Pookie was lapping up a large bowl of near-nectar concocted by Frau Schuylkill. Octavius said to all and sundry. "That effort will cause a temporary lapse in the General's efforts but he's not going to quit. He's a single-minded fanatic. I realize Heaven doesn't want to countenance his assassination but we need to get him and Moriarty safely imprisoned somewhere before they can recoup their losses. What are we going to do about Moriarty back on Earth Beta?"

Juliet said, "I was hoping we could convince Holmes that the professor's not dead and you and he could exile him somewhere permanently. Hopefully we can do the same with the General but he's a tougher case since he has resources to flit, *(or does he zap?)* throughout the Cosmos."

She turned to the otter. Sir Otto, could you assist me in convincing Holmes to take on Moriarty? Doctor Bear, care for a little time traveling?"

"OK , but Moriarty is less of a threat now that the General is for the moment at least, without his invasion force. I want to spend a little time with my team plotting how to put the crazy horse out of business permanently."

Otto gave the Baroness one of his goofy grins. He was sitting next to his Tarot partner. "At your service, Lady Juliet, just as soon as Madame Giselle and I do our television show. We're leaving for New York in the morning, will do our act in the evening and be back late next day. Say, would you and your dog, Pookie, like to come with us? She'd be a sensational addition to our act. She looks like Giselle's twin sister and she's a fabulous flyer and dancer."

Giselle Woof nodded her turbaned head, clapped her paws in delight and barked. "Oh Splendide! Magnifique! Merveilleux! Incroyable! Fantastique!"

The otter laughed. "I take it you think it's a good idea."

"Certainment! What do you think, Baroness. As an H.sap, you'd be a shock but Mlle Pookie would be a marvel. Will you two come?"

Pookie, who is nonverbal but understands language and conversations very well, had just finished off her bowl of pseudo-nectar. She looked over at Juliet and then stood on her hind legs, pirouetted over to the Otter and Giselle and leapt into the air, growling as she rose. She landed back on her forepaws, flipped and bowed to the laughter and applause.

Juliet laughed, "I wouldn't want to be presumptuous here but I suspect she thinks it's a good idea. All right. Let's give my canine companion her opportunity for stardom on Earth Alpha TV. I'm sure we can wait a day or two now that General Turmoil has been momentarily stalled. Doctor Bear, Colonel, Frau, Howard and Bearoness, can we have an all hands strategy session when I return."

The Great Bear agreed. "It's time we got Sherlock Holmes involved. I trust you can set that up, Lady Juliet."

"I plan to approach him first and then I'd like you, Sir Otto and the Ursulas to assist me in getting him to deal with Moriarty. Our first task is convincing Holmes that the Professor is still alive. We'll also have to get him to believe Earth Alpha exists and General Turmoil is still a real threat. He simply refers to Earth Beta as Earth, Other worlds and exoplanets are outside his experience. He may even believe the Earth is flat."

Octavius laughed, "Really?"

"Yes, it took him a while to accept the existence of Heaven, even in the face of evidence. For a consummate genius, Holmes has his blind spots. Oddly, Doctor Watson, whose intellect, while impressive, doesn't match Holmes, is more aware of the natural state of things. I'll enlist his aid."

"Meanwhile, I'm looking forward to this television experience. We had no such thing on Earth Beta. Music Hall and Theatres galore! I trod the boards in many of them but performing for an audience of millions spread all over the world. That's unheard of. I hope it doesn't go to Pookie's head. She's a lovable but extremely vain little creature. But super talented. It's a pity you can't see her perform with the Lipizzaner stallions and Pegasus. They're marvels. And she's a top notch aerobatic flyer. She's quite good at Multi-Dimensional Fetch, a game I'll never understand."

The dog was listening to all of this, barked and stood on her hind legs and bowed. She was obviously ready for her next theatrical triumph.

Chapter Seven

Right after dawn, a De Havilland Canada DHC-6 Twin Otter Classic 300-G had been towed from its assigned slot in the Octavian Roman Temple and was being fueled and checked out by the ground staff. Today's flight crew consisted of Frau Ilse Schuylkill and Colonel Wyatt Where *(US Army Retired).* The flying warhorse had a light passenger load. Giselle Woof, Sir Otto. Maury Meerkat *(their talent agent)* Chita *(their producer/director)* Baroness Juliet and Pookie both in their materialized forms and the Twins - Arabella and McTavish. The angels were on board.

Juliet was charmed. She settled back in the bear sized seat next to Chita and said, "This is a new experience. These kinds of aircraft haven't appeared yet on Earth Beta and we don't need them in Heaven although the angels have their chariots. We've been in balloons and airships but nothing like this. Pookie and I just flit wherever we want to go but I thought we'd keep you company as we go to New York. We haven't been to a 21st century Earth Alpha city like the Big Apple. Why is it called that?"

Chita replied. "I looked it up once. New York City's nickname has nothing to do with fruit production. In fact, the Big Apple moniker first gained popularity in connection with horseracing. Around 1920, a New York City newspaper reporter, heard stable hands in New Orleans say they were going to "the big apple," a reference to New York City, whose race tracks were considered big-time venues. In the 1930s, jazz musicians adopted the term to indicate New York City was home to big-league music clubs. After a hiatus, the name regained popularity in the 70's."

The Baroness laughed, "You're a font of information!"

The cheetah chirped, "Yeah, most of it is useless but it's part of my job being Octavius' Publicity Director. Don't get the Twins started on New York. They love the place and look for every opportunity to get up there."

The Baroness said, "I'll control my enthusiasm."

The cat looked at Juliet. "You can add to my useless knowledge reserve, if you will."

"Try me!"

"I'm an American but I spend a great deal of my time In England. London more often than not."

"Earth Alpha London!"

"Right you are, Baroness. Certainly different from the smoky town where you spent your life. I understand you were something of a show-biz sensation."

"I had my moments. Singing, dancing, stage romancing! 'Jolly Juliet', if you can believe it."

Chita laughed, "I perform as Miss Catt. Dignified name, rowdy persona! I understand you married into high society. A baron?"

"One of the greater mistakes of my life. Reginald, Baron Crestwell was a cad and a jerk. But he was rich and a peer. However, our marriage was short lived. I was shot and to my surprise, ended up in Heaven's climes. I still don't know why I was directly admitted. Mary, the Queen of Heaven seems to have had a hand in it. Anyway, I insisted I wouldn't enter Paradise until Sherlock Holmes and I found out who killed me. The powers-that-be gave in and so did Holmes who wasn't enthralled with prospect. That's how the Consulting Detective and I became partners. We solved the mystery and I took up my delightful afterlife in heaven. I was reunited with Pookie, my charming and super-clever dog and we live in a magnificent celestial mansion along with some members of the Lipizzaner stallion troupe and would you believe, a unicorn and Pegasus the flying horse. I still keep up an active association with Holmes, much to the chagrin of the Celestial Governing Committee."

The cat shook her head in disbelief. "You certainly are something else. So, you're going to use your partnership to get Holmes to deal with the Moriarty character."

"I hope so. He and Doctor Watson have had several rounds with the Professor. Holmes thinks he's dead. I'm counting on the Octavian's help to prove he's wrong. Moriarty is alive and dangerous. But enough about me. You had a question."

"Yeah. This whole monarchy and peerage business. It's still around after all this time. As you know we don't have royalty, nobility and the like in America and I keep sticking my social paw in it when I'm in England. I understand it's mostly a European thing with a few exceptions like Japan. You're a noble. How does it work?"

"Well, distinct social classes are far more important on Earth Beta than in your world. We have kings, queens, emperors and empresses galore all over the planet. As best I can tell, they're slowly but definitely fading away on Earth

Alpha. Although as you suggest, the United Kingdom is still holding on. You have a king, queen and a large batch of princes and princesses."

"I know about them. It's the lower levels that have me confused. Peers of the Realm.The House of Lords and the hereditary nobility. I never know who trumps whom. Who do I say 'milord and milady' to? Am I supposed to curtsey to these animals. Take the Bearoness for example. She's a pal. I'd never think of calling her Your Ladyship or Madam. And she'd probably swat me if I curtseyed. How do you want me to address you?"

"Juliet will do very nicely, thank you. Well, it can get rather complex and I can see your dilemma. Let me give you the short course. In England, there is a definite pecking order of the nobles below the royalty. Some are very sticky about it. There are plenty of snobs in both our worlds. Others couldn't care less. Who sits where at dinner and who is served first is still an issue. If a peer gets arrested, he or she has the right to be judged by the House of Lords. The sentences, if any, are usually light. I think it's stupid but who am I. A lowly baroness."

"A _LOWLY_ baroness? You're kidding!"

"Oh yes, both Belinda and I are quite a way down the totem pole. Let me spell it out. On top of the peer heap live the Dukes and Duchesses. They're below royalty but well above the other nobles and of course, the commoners. Not many of them. They're addressed as Your Grace. Males bow to them. Females curtsey.

Chita chirped. "Can you imagine me doing a curtsey with these long legs of mine. I'd topple over."

Juliet laughed. "I'm pretty clumsy when it comes to curtseying even though I was a dancer. Now, Pookie, the little show off, can do bows, curtseys and backflips to perfection. Anyway, next down in rank are the Marquesses and Marchionesses. You won't see too many of them. When you do, it's My Lord or My Lady."

"Number three on the tree are the Earls and Countesses. On the continent, the term 'Count' applies. 'Countess" is always used everywhere. No one wants to be called an 'Earless.' They're addressed as My Lord and My Lady."

"Number four in our peer parade are the Viscounts and Viscountesses. It's 'Vycount'. You don't pronounce the 's.' They too are My Lord and My Lady."

"We finally arrive at the lowest grade of the peerage. The Baron. A wife of a Baron is styled as a Baroness. That's Belinda and me. We get the Milady treatment, too."

"There are two other titles that are not considered part of the peerage. Baronet and Knight. They are addressed as Sir and Lady. Does all this help?"

The cat sighed. "OK! I understand the 'what'. What I don't get is the 'why."

"It's human and animal nature to one-up your neighbor and lord it over him or her. Sheer snobbery. For centuries. Not very popular in heaven although we do have a few souls who persist in pulling rank. They don't get far with it. Let's change the subject. Tell me about this aeroplane."

Chita, who wasn't very fond of flying even though she did quite a lot of it, replied. "Well, the seats are comfortable, the galley is fully stocked and there are two loos although I don't know if you need them or not. This plane is slow compared to the jets but it flies smoothly enough. Unfortunately, the propeller engines are noisy so don't expect to have peaceful conversations."

As usual Arabella and McTavish were busy with an Ursula, working on their latest electronic game. They were hoping to snag Juliet as one of their game characters. Orifiel was seated invisibly in the rear of the aircraft along with the Octavians' guardians angels.

Pookie was sitting with Otto and Giselle, nodding as they outlined their routine and how the heavenly dog would fit into it. Laughter and barks of delight as they came up with more and more 'shtick.'

The destination was Teterboro Airport and ultimately Manhattan at the studios of WTWT, home of Bernie's Big Variety Show on nationwide TV. They were booked for a twenty minute performance.

Frau Schuylkill's commanding voice echoed over the intercom, telling all and sundry to buckle up, stow loose materials and sit back for takeoff. The turboprop engines whined and switched to a roar as the Twin Otter hurtled down the runway and made its way into the morning Ohio air. They were off. A bit more than two hours in the practically cloudless skies over Ohio, Pennsylvania and New Jersey until they arrived at their airport destination. Juliet was fascinated. Even here in the East, the United States had so much open space. Of course, Heaven had limitless space. She was looking forward to her return to Paradise, her mansion, the Lipizzaners and her celestial friends.

On the other hand, she will welcome more Earth time with Sherlock Holmes, Doctor Watson and Mrs. Hudson. She could do without Scotland Yard.

When the seatbelt light went off, Chita uncurled from her seat and strode back to the galley. She returned with a tray of snacks and two flutes of champagne. She howled. "I had to beat those kids to the food or there wouldn't be any left. Teen age snarfing machines! I'm sure the show's producers will lay out a fabulous dinner for us. These TV people live on the high end of the hog."

And so it went. The performers had worked out their routine with Pookie joining Otto in a classic dance and acrobatic routine while Giselle pretended to be annoyed. The twins had added several AI apps to their newest game – *Bears in the Air.* Maury was on the phone to the studio working out last minute modifications to the performance including the inclusion of Pookie. "She's Giselle's younger sister. She doesn't talk but she dances up a storm and flies in the process, You'll love her and the best part is there's no extra charge for her participation. Tell Bernie! He'll be delighted."

Bernie was a Bernese Mountain Dog who had hosted the Bernie's Big Variety Show *(BBVS)* for what seemed like centuries. He nicknamed it Bernie's Blockbuster Varieties. Maury had placed Bearnice and Bearyl Blanc on several of his programs. Bernie came across to his audience as a gracious sweetheart. Off camera, he was anything but. Snarling at producers, directors, technicians, musicians, studio writers and talent, he made himself generally obnoxious. But his viewers loved him and the show was rated very highly since he booked terrific and unusual acts like Otto and Giselle. He also paid his guests well, treating them to a wide range of amenities like fabulous meals and the limos that were waiting at the airport for the Octavians.

The Twin Otter descended through the Jersey skies. The towers of New York City were off in the distance. The twins had put aside their Ursula recorders and were sitting with noses pressed against the plane's windows, pointing out the skyscrapers they recognized. The buildings disappeared below the horizon as the airplane with full flaps extended, touched down on the short VTOL runway. They taxied to the reserved aircraft parking area and shut down the whining turboprops.

Two limos were standing by with liveried drivers. The first was ready to take the 'talent' plus Maury and Chita to the studios. The second would wait for the Frau and Colonel to close out the Twin Otter, see to its refueling and sign all the paper work for overnight storage. The Twins would ride with them.

Juliet and Pookie went invisibly in the first limo along with the angels, leaving room in the car for the mortals. Off they went down the Jersey highways, through the Lincoln Tunnel, into the Manhattan traffic-smothered streets and on to the TV studio where a sumptuous dinner and Bernie awaited. As soon as they arrived, she and Pookie materialized to the puzzlement of the driver. She petted the dog, whispered to her and went invisible once more but the Bichon stayed solid. As an H.sap, Juliet would have set off a riot.

A uniformed page led them to an elevator and into the studio. Bernie Bernese was standing in front of a couch and pointing threateningly at a large Akita wearing a headset and carrying a clipboard. "You heard me, Axel. You're fired! Pack your things and get out. Turn your stuff over to Gloria. She'll direct tonight's taping." He noticed the procession coming into the room and recognized the Meerkat. A phony smile lit up his face. "Maury, sweetheart, so glad to see you. This is the Tarot act you promised me? Two Bichons? Is that your star's understudy?"

Maury smiled, "No, she's Pookie, Madame Giselle's kid sister. Very shy. Doesn't talk much but she's an absolutely spectacular dancer. I told your director Axel about her."

"Yeah, well I just fired Axel. Incompetent jerk! He didn't tell me. I didn't realize your Madame Giselle dances.

"She doesn't but her partner, Otto the Magnificent does among other slapstick routines. He and Pookie have worked up some routines to lighten up the act. Otto, Pookie. Give Bernie a sample."

The otter bounced onstage, spun in tight circles, flipped and did a split. Pookie jumped on his shoulders, danced on top of his head and the two of them ended with a series of synchronized somersaults. They both turned and pointed at Madame Giselle who made a solemn entrance in front of the couch. While Pookie strutted on her hind legs, Otto juggled a deck of Tarot cards, threw them in the air and stood back as they settled into Giselle's paws."

Maury said, "That's just part of the intro. Then she does her predictions with members of the audience. I assume you tape in front of a live audience."

Bernie and the surrounding staff were laughing and applauding. All except Axel who with his face like a thundercloud, threw his headset across the studio and stomped off. Bernie looked after him, shrugged and answered Maury's question, "We tape at seven and broadcast at eleven. That gives us time to deal with any glitches and leave space for the commercials."

"Fine, let me introduce Chita, She works with Otto and the dogs to design the act."

The cat had watched the Akita make his dramatic exit and then turned to Bernie. "I have Giselle's music and their costumes. We're going to need some members of the audience for Giselle to interview and make predictions. Three pair will do."

Bernie called an alpaca over. "Gloria, do we have those animals picked out and briefed."

"Yes Bernie", she lisped. "All ready and willing. A female computer programmer, a stock broker, a cop, a chef and pair of sister librarians."

"Fantastic! It's five o'clock! Let's eat and then we'll rehearse with the band."

The invisible Baroness and angels were carefully watching all of this. Lady Juliet had, of course, never been in an Earth Alpha television studio. Angelic Communications used a form of media somewhat similar but without all the cables, sets, cameras, microphones, headsets, monitors, speakers, teleprompters and house band. In Heaven, the celestial images just appeared and the music rose in the background. This was different.

*****

The rehearsal had gone well. The pre-selected volunteers were suitably briefed by Chita. Pookie and Otto had the cast and crew in stitches. At six fifteen, the audience was admitted to the studio for the taping. Promptly at seven, the house lights in the packed theatre dimmed and a drum roll grew in volume and speed. Bernie, ever the genial host, sprang onstage and after some introductory patter in which he botched Madame Giselle's name he sat at his desk delivering a trite monologue. He and the band leader exchanged some small talk. Juliet was not impressed. Then the moment of truth.

Bernie smiled and said, "I've never believed in the Tarot but tonight's guest performers have me changing my mind. I'm also amazed at their impossible antics. Ladies and Gentlebeasts, please welcome the Tarot Trio!"

Juliet winced and looked at Chita, "Oh, brother! Where did he get that name from?"

Another drum roll and rim shot and Otto "zapped' onstage from nowhere and executed a series of backflips ending in a kneeling bow with arms spread as the brass exploded with an exciting fanfare. Ta-Da! Wild applause. "How did he do that? Where did he come from?" The Octavians knew, The audience didn't. A moment later, Pookie rose from her chair, executed a series of tricks with the otter and skipped off stage, ready to re-enter with Giselle.

"Ladies and Gentlebeasts," Otto shouted, "Welcome to the world of the Tarot. I am obviously not Madame Giselle. *(Laughter)* As you've probably concluded, I am Hairy Otter, known in some circles as Sir Otto the Magnificent. We're delighted you've chosen to join us this evening. We are prepared to awe and entertain you."

He bowed again and straightened his red satin jacket. "Now, let me introduce the mysterious mistress of cartomancy, Madame Giselle, Queen of the Tarot. And her assistant, Ms. Pookie."

The band played an exotic oriental melody as Giselle made her entrance, bathed in a 'follow' spotlight. Clad in a sparkling gold lamé robe with a small matching turban perched between her ears, she was trailed by Pookie in a silver version of the same costume. They bowed to the audience's enthusiastic applause, nodded to Otto and proceeded to the elaborately decorated table and chairs positioned in the center of the stage. Ursula 18, the new experimental model, was standing by offstage, unnoticed by the cast and crew, ready to feed Giselle with information on her next client through augmented reality contact lenses. Once Pookie did several high flying spins and Giselle was seated, Otto looked at her and asked, "Madame, are the spirits active tonight?"

"Mais Oui, Monsieur Otto. They are quite eager to help our studio friends reach new wisdom."

"Well, let's begin!"

"Will you fetch the cards for me, please?"

Suddenly a cascade of cards *(under Otto's telekinetic control)* tumbled out of the air and landed in a neat stack in front of Pookie. She in turn swept them up with one paw. raised them *(again under Ottos' control)* and floated the deck through the air to Giselle. (Ooohs and aaahs from the audience.)

She barked, "Very clever, Mes Amis. M'sieur Otto, shall I do a quick reading for you?"

"Of course, make a prediction."

"First you must cut and shuffle the cards."

The deck rose from the table, broke into two halves, shuffled itself and settled back on the surface, face down. *(Amazed laughter)*

He chortled, "There! So much easier to let them do it themselves. You know what a klutz I am."

"Indeed, let me take a moment to explain the Tarot deck for those in the audience who are not familiar with it." She gave a short tutorial and then waved Otto into the other chair next to Pookie.

"You have just returned from several journeys, am I correct?"

"Unfortunately, yes!"

"Let us see if the cards have anything to say about that. As you know, the Tarot is also known as the Fool's Journey."

"Well, I'm certainly the Fool."

"Oui! Indeed, you are. I shall take 3 cards." She flipped the top card. "Ah, Here is the Fool. Let us take the next card. Voila! The Chariot. Your journey begins. And now the third card. The Wheel of Fortune. Are you ready to embark and bring fortune with you?"

He disappeared. *(zapped)* Murmurs throughout the audience. Suddenly a squeaky voice resonated from the back of the room. The cameras and microphones picked him up. "Here I am, Madame. Journey's end. I have your first seeker ready to join you." Pookie flew to the pair. Amazed stares from the onlookers. "Go with Pookie, please, Miss."

She led a slender female gazelle up to the stage. The otter arrived onstage a moment later. "Madame *Giselle*. This is Ms. Gaby *Gazelle*. She seeks your guidance."

"Thank you, Otto. Please be seated Ms. Gazelle. Have we ever met or do we have mutual acquaintances?"

"Oh no! I just arrived today. This is my first trip to New York. I don't know either of you."

"D'accord!" A message flashed across her contact lenses. Ursula 18 on the job. "She's a data specialist on vacation, by herself and looking for romance."

"Am I correct that you are here alone?"

"Yes! I'm on vacation."

"Away from all those large databases, computers and annoying software."

"How did you know I'm involved in databases?"

"The spirits informed me. Now let us see what is in store for you."

She handed the deck to the gazelle who rather skillfully cut and shuffled the cards and gave them back.

Giselle chuckled. "I see you are a card player." She peeled off and laid out three cards. She turned them over slowly and said, "I see an important change in your life. A pleasant change. You will find romance soon."

Gaby gasped, clasped Giselle's paw and stepped backward on the stage. Otto was on the side of the room with a large antelope male in tow. Once more the cameras picked them up. "Madame Giselle, meet Mister Antwell." Ursula flashed on Giselle's contact lenses. "Single, rich, stockbroker, British aristocracy, son of an earl, here on business, socially unskilled."

"Bon Soir, Monsieur or should I call you Milord? You are the son of an earl, are you not."

He reacted in amazement. "It's true but I don't use the title. Actually I'm a second son."

"But your elder brother is no longer alive?"

"Unfortunately, no!"

"So Milord, What can the spirits help you with?"

"I don't know. I'd just like something new in my life."

"Perhaps, *someone* new?"

"Well, yes!"

"Let us see!" She handed him the deck which he also skillfully shuffled and cut.

Otto chuckled. "Had some experience with cards, eh?"

"A bit." He placed the deck face down and Giselle picked off the top three cards.

"It seems you have attracted the ladies. The Queen of Wands, the Queen of Swords and the Empress. All good signs of a blossoming relationship."

Otto leaned over and said. "May I introduce you two. Your lordship, meet Gaby. Gaby meet the Earl. You're both a pair of cardsharps." Laughter and applause as the two of them left the stage.

And so it went. Otto and Pookie amazing the audience with their slapstick tricks, Giselle pretending annoyance at their antics and reading the Tarot cards for four more members of the audience.

Finally the band started to play Giselle's exit music. She rose and bowed. "Mesdames and Messieurs. Merci Beaucoup! Tu aussi, Monsieur Bernie. My associates and I are so pleased that you all have joined us this evening. I hope you feel the spirits made our little offering entertaining and valuable. Thank you again. Au Revoir. Be careful going home. Say goodnight, Otto!"

"Goodnight Otto!" Hairy Otter sent the Tarot deck flying into the air, executed several back flips in sync with Pookie and caught the cards in a stack before they fell to the floor. The crowd went wild.

A standing ovation as the three of them took several bows while the band continued to play their exit music.

Suddenly, several shots were fired from the back of the room. Bernie fell over holding his forepaw. Screams and growls. The audience was dumbstruck and motionless. Chita leaped from her seat in the front and sprinted toward the would-be assailant. It was Alex, the recently fired Director.

Waving a pistol, he turned toward the rear door of the room and ran back. He was no match for the high speed cat who tackled him and sat on top of him. The gun went skittering along the floor. Two hefty gorillas from TV station security pounced on him, cuffed him and hauled him out of the room. The Akita kept shouting, "I'll kill the bastard. He's humiliated me for the last time."

Chita swiftly disappeared, leaving the authorities to deal with the situation and the production team to do some fast editing to eliminate the attack. The audience was quickly escorted out. At eleven, they would show the Tarot act and then switch to a review of Bernie's up coming programs. Alex was on his way to jail. Giselle, Otto and Pookie were helped by Maury and the Twins in putting all their paraphernalia back in the boxes. A doctor in the audience had bandaged Bernie's flesh wound while he complained loudly.

He came over to Maury and the "Tarot Trio" and said, "Well, your act was sensational but not quite up to my being shot. Was that cheetah with you? She's gone! We're going to show the attack on the late evening news. Bernie Bernese assaulted by a disgruntled producer! You can't buy that kind of exposure. Never miss an opportunity for publicity. This business is all about ratings." The Meerkat resisted punching him in the mouth but just wanted to get out of there. So did the whole team.

Next morning, Chita showed up for breakfast to the applause of the team. "Great job, Ms. Catt although I thought seriously of shooting that creep, myself. I hope they go easy on Alex."

"Thanks, Maury. Maybe I should have just let him go but the way he was waving that gun around, someone else was going to get hurt."

The Twins yelped, "You're a heroine, Chita. You're going to have a big time part in our next game – *Bears in the Air.*

Once the wait staff had left the room, Juliet materialized. She congratulated the cat. She was eager to get back to the Twin Otter and get out of New York.

After a quick breakfast, the trip back to the Bear's Lair was uneventful except for several traffic delays on the roads to the airport. The Twin Otter had been refueled and prepped and the team piled in. Giselle and Otto were worn out from their performance. Pookie, being immortal, showed no signs of weariness and watched the scenery as the plane took off and headed southwest for Cincinnati. Arabella and McTavish had been reluctant to leave New York but once on board, busied themselves with adding last night's adventure to their newest game. The angels were seated in the rear of the aircraft where they took up no space and added no weight. They had been stirred into action during the shooting but relieved that no harm had come to the Octavians. Maury was gently snoring in his oversized seat.

Chita and Juliet had struck up a friendship in the last 48 hours and were comparing notes. The cat lived in London when she wasn't traveling between Polar Paradise in the Shetlands and the Bear's Lair. She and the Baroness were bringing each other up to date on the differences of Old Blighty and London on Earths Alpha and Beta. Juliet gave Chita some interesting insights on what the Victorians were actually like. They were both singers and midway through the flight they crooned a couple of old standards they both knew. The Baroness' contralto blended with the cheetah's chirps, growls, trills and yips, keeping time on the tray tables in front of them. Applause from the passengers and laughter from the pair.

Maury had awakened and was listening to the pair. " Baroness, is there any way we can team the two of you up. Bearnice Blanc, my singing polar protégé has been knocking them dead worldwide but I'd be delighted to represent the two of you on the musical stages."

"Maury, thanks, but you can see how impossible that would be. One of us is very much alive and the other is very much deceased. On top of that, how would an H.sap go over in an all animal world or a Cheetah in the 1905 London Music Halls. It's fun but it's a non-starter."

Chita purred. "Speaking of non-starters, I can't get over that jerk Bernie Bernese. Talk about a nasty no-talent egotist. Those kind give show-biz a bad name but he certainly has the audience."

The Baroness agreed. "He's a highly polished hypocrite. He's going to milk that wound for all it's worth and then some. I feel sorry for poor Alex. The dog was clearly over the edge in frustration. But shooting your enemy is no solution even if we do it so gratuitously in war."

That last thought set the Baroness off on a private meditation. This assignment had too much violence associated with it and they hadn't even dealt personally with General Turmoil or Moriarty yet. Although destroying their engines of war was no small task. She needed to consult with Magdalen.

They touched down at the mansion and were greeted by Octavius and Belinda. "We watched the show on Late Night TV. The Tarot Trio were terrific.

What about the shooting? That phony Bernie Bernese is all over the airwaves with his tale of woe. It's a shame he was only wounded."

The Baroness laughed. "Octavius, Belinda. I have to return to Heaven to confer with mu superiors. Pookie and I *(and the angels)* will be back shortly. We still have to deal with the General and Moriarty and we have to convince Holmes that the Professor is still alive."

The Great Bear snorted. "Well, we're at your disposal. I'm looking forward to a trip to Earth Beta and meeting the famous Sherlock Holmes. I'm sure that together we can deal with our adversaries. We should probably just dump the both of them into that star. They deserve it."

"Sorry, Octavius. The Queen of Heaven insists on keeping them alive but unable to inflict their vicious mischief."

"That presents some real difficulties. Lady Mary is far more merciful than I am."

"That's why she's the Queen of Heaven."

Chapter Eight

"Congratulations, Juliet. The Queen is very pleased with your destruction of the General's engines of war. However, we both know that will only slow them down and not deter them from their insane plans." Magdalen and Lady Juliet sat in the orangery of the Baroness' Mansion sipping delicious cups of nectar. Pookie had devoured a ration of Heavenly Chewies and had just stretched out for her morning siesta. Earthly show business could be very tiring even for an immortal dog although she really enjoyed cavorting with Otto and Giselle. Maybe she could squeeze in a game of Multi-Dimensional Fetch with her pals in the Meadows before having to return to Earth Alpha. She'd also go and see her friends, the Lipizzaners.

The two women stared at each other. Magda spoke. "I know it's difficult dealing with those scoundrels and not being able to kill them off or do them extreme bodily harm. Mercy is sometimes very hard to maintain. But even the most despicable people have the right to live out their natural lives."

"Even if they seek to end the lives of so many others? That bothers me but who am I to protest. Well, what do you and the Queen suggest?"

"Enforced Exile!"

"Together?"

"Oh, heavens, No! Those two would just feed off each other. Trick them into irretrievable banishment. There are millions of exoplanets and such where they can while away their lives in misery. In a sense it's the worst form of letting them survive. A living Torment. Perhaps they may even repent."

"I sincerely doubt that! I believe they'll end up in Hell. Satan can deal with them."

"I guess I agree but we have to give them the opportunity. Although I doubt they'll take advantage of it."

"All right. After a brief visit with Empress Sisi, Mr. Sherman, the Lipis, Pegasus and Hugh, the Unicorn, I'll return to Earth Alpha and Octavius and his crew. Then we'll visit Holmes, convince him of the General's existence and the fact that the Professor is still alive. Then we'll all figure out how to get the General and Moriarty out of circulation. Finally, I want to return to Heaven. This adventure has become a bit much for me."

"Wonderful! You're in our prayers."

"I can use all the help I can get."

She rose and flitted around to the magnificent stables where the splendid snowy horses awaited. Pookie pranced along with her. Der Alte, wonderful stallion that he was, emerged from his stall, whickered and nuzzled the Baroness. Pookie jumped on his back and they paraded around the paddock. As Juliet walked along the stalls, patting the pure white steeds, she heard a thundering, flapping noise. Pegasus with Empress Sisi astride, settled down in the paddock next to Pookie and Der Alte.

"Welcome back, Juliet. Are you here to stay? How did your earthbound adventures play out?"

"Sisi, my dear! No, my earthbound adventures are still in progress. I came back here to consult with Mary Magdalen and now after a brief break, Pookie and I are once again leaving Paradise for a different one - Polar Paradise, a resort in Scotland, *(the Shetlands to be exact)* presided over by another Baroness – I should say Bearoness - Belinda Béarnaise Bruin Bear (nee Black). She's Octavius Bear's wife. I've been involved in a major effort to frustrate the plans of two major criminals to conquer the universe."

The Empress laughed, "Oh well, nothing too important, then. Mr. Sherman and I have been standing by with the animals in case you needed any help but so far things have been quiet inside the Pearly Gates." She looked over at Pookie still cavorting with Der Alte and asked, "How is our little friend doing?"

"You'll be surprised to know that Pookie has become a star of television on Earth Alpha."

"Television? What's that?"

"It's like our Heavenly message and entertainment service. Only they use electronic technology to broadcast what they call shows, segments and endless commercial sales pitches. Silly things! Don't ask me to explain the tools they use. Earth Alpha is far ahead of our old stamping grounds when it comes to science and engineering. But they still have their share of crime and criminals. Octavius Bear and his associates, the Octavians, are first class crime fighters among other things."

She continued, "Oh, tell Hugh, he's not the only Unicorn in existence. There's another live one who runs a pub near this castle Pookie and I are going to. He's a partner with a Lion, if you can credit it. Give my best to my parents and brother. I'll stop by to see them when we return and I'll bring you all up to date on our exploits. Pookie, come dear! Earth Alpha and the Octavians await."

The dog jumped down from the stallion's back and yelped as she backed into the Heavenly Director, Raymond. "God's blessings on you, Baroness and on your little dog. I have just spoken with Mary Magdalen and Queen Mary. They are quite pleased with your progress so far. It seems Octavius Bear and his associates are quite formidable. Their brief sojourn in Heaven seems to have convinced them of their celestial mission even though they no longer remember being here. Sending the General's weapons and facilities crashing into that star was a neat piece of work. However, I'm sure both of our opponents are enraged by the attack. They will not stand by idly. If and when they seek revenge, remember the Queen would prefer no lives are lost. I know that sounds unfair to you but mercy and compassion extend even to the worst sinners."

"It does make things more difficult, Raymond. It certainly limits our options but I certainly will not disobey the Queen. Pookie and I are on our way back to Earth Alpha where we will briefly confer with Octavius and then on to my Earth Beta teammate, Sherlock Holmes. We have to convince him Earth Alpha exists, that Professor Moriarty is still alive and along with General Turmoil is threatening the universe, even though their war machine has been temporarily destroyed. A solid day's work. I'm looking forward to getting it over with and coming back to relax over a hearty meal of nectar and ambrosia."

"The angels and I are looking out for you. Blessings and Godspeed!"

*****

Meanwhile, after returning from New York, the Octavians had traveled from the Bear's Lair to the Shetlands and Polar Paradise. In order to retain her Bearonial status, Belinda had to reside in Scotland for six months of the year. She spent that time managing the palace/resort and overseeing the port-of-call franchise she had negotiated with the Solar Seas Cruise Line. Every two weeks the **North Wind,** a cruise ship specially fitted our for near Arctic sailing, arrived at Polar Paradise and its new sea terminal to unload cold loving tourists and pick up re-embarking vacationers. Between the helicopter and ferry service from Abeardeen and the ocean going cruise traffic, Polar Paradise had become a very popular place. It kept winning awards for hospitality, comfort, entertainment, food and drink from the most prestigious tourist ratings bodies. Hotel Manager Ms. Fairbearn; Polar Paradise Executive Dougal; Security Managers Lord David and Dancing Dan; Water Activities Manager Harold; Fiona, Directress of Lion and Unicorn Enterprises; Executive Chef Mrs. McRadish and the cloned sheep waitresses (Holly, Molly, Polly and Dolly) all worked their magic to keep the resort at the highest standards of quality and enjoyment.

In a few weeks, Belinda and Octavius were to be witnesses at the murder trial of Polonius Polar in the Shetlands municipality of Lerwick. He had posed as her father seeking to get a major share of her wealth. A little DNA research disproved that assertion. He is accused of killing his secretary, Paul, who was blackmailing him. *(See Book 20 of the Casebooks of Octavius Bear.)*

So, off the Baroness went with Pookie to Bearmoral to participate in the next round of the Cosmic Endgames.

"Pookie, I've never seen so many polar bears in my entire life or afterlife." Lady Juliet and her canine companion had flitted from Heaven's gates to the gates of Polar Paradise in Bearmoral. Arriving invisibly, they stood in the resort courtyard as the tourists debarked from the *North Wind* which had just arrived. Two processions of incomers and outgoers led up to and down between the hotel's drawbridge and lobby and the ship terminal. Lord David, Dancing Dan and Jaguar Jack along with the ship's social and security staff were processing the lines and seeing to luggage and last minute issues.

The sun was shining but a cold wind whipped across the property. The choppy waves in the bay seemed to appeal to the polar cubs who had run off from their parents waiting on the lines. Several of them were jumping back and forth as the surf rolled toward the shore. Although she didn't feel the cold or the wet, Juliet still shivered. Pookie, barking silently, running and flitting with an occasional backflip, chased the breakers.

"Well, I'm glad we don't have to join that group. Although they all seem happy enough. Come, Pookie! Let's flit into the lobby and up to the Bearoness' suite on the penthouse floor. Some of the Octavians should be waiting for us. Come with, Orifiel."

Unseen, they flew over the drawbridge and past the crowded front desk. Bearoness Belinda was standing with the sheepdog Dougal and the polar Ms. Fairbearn observing and occasionally participating in the registration process, welcoming newcomers and paying special attention to returning guests. Not all the tourists were polar bears. Arctic foxes, caribou, reindeer, musk oxen, two walruses, four seals and all the way from the South Pole, a waddle of penguins were signing in. Cubs and juveniles scampered around the lobby, jumping on the furniture and adding to the general noise level.

Passing up the busy elevators, Juliet, Pookie and the angel flew to the top floor. The two of them materialized in the Bearonial suite where Maury Meerkat, Frau Ilse, Howard, the Colonel and Chita were gathered. Hugs and shouts of greetings. Octavius rambled into the room and greeted Juliet. "Welcome back, Baroness and you too, Pookie. Glad to see both of you. It seems we have some unfinished business to attend to. Ursula, ask Belinda to join us. I'm sure she'll welcome the opportunity to escape from that crowd downstairs. Every time that ship arrives, we have several hours of bedlam. But it's great for business."

"Hello all." Juliet chuckled. "Long time, no see! Do you spend more time in the air than on the ground? Another long flight, although I assume this one was supersonic. Mach something? Who was Mach anyway?"

Howard, ever the scientist, responded, "Ernst Mach was an Austrian physicist and philosopher, who contributed to the physics of shock waves. The ratio of the speed of a flow or object to that of sound is named the Mach number in his honor. And yes, we do make a number of long distance flights. International, intercontinental, interplanetary, intergalactic. We haven't made it to Heaven yet, but we'll give it a try."

Juliet looked at Maury and Octavius and thought to herself, "Little does Howard know."

She picked a flute of champagne off the serving table and said, "We passed Belinda in the lobby playing super-hostess."

"She's very good at it. She also insists that the entire resort must be always up to the highest standards – from accommodations to food to entertainment to sports. We have a sizeable number of return guests. That has to tell you something. She also serves on the Board of the Solar Seas Cruise Line. She has been taking steps to ensure they evince quality in everything they do. I sometimes think they're afraid of her. But they're doing very well. We took a Caribbean tour on their eco super ship, *The Solar Wind*. What a wonderful vessel. Unfortunately it was also the scene of several crimes and hefty tropical storm. Needless to say, the Twins loved it."

"How are our young friends?"

"Energetic as ever. They're busy on their next electronic game – *Bears in the Air.* They keep the Ursulas and the Hexagon Deep Data Center busy."

"Someday I'd like to actually visit the center instead of a video link. I'm a technological nincompoop but I'm fascinated by the scientific and mathematical strides Earth Alpha has made and you folks seem to be in the vanguard."

Howard grinned. "We need to get you together with Condo, Byzz and their staff in the flesh. They'll put on quite a show for you. Of course, I'm sure you heavenly immortals have no real need for all of our bells and whistles. And not all the techie stuff is for the good. Witness our worthy or not so worthy opponents, Turmoil and Moriarty. The worst of Earths Alpha and Beta."

The Baroness shook her head in agreement. "I was amazed, Howard, in your ability to move those buildings and equipment through space and into that star. Could you have moved the entire exoplanet?"

"Sorry, Baroness. That's beyond our equipment's strength and capabilities. We were pushing the limits. Although we could have slowly torn the place apart and sent the pieces for a ride. It would have taken weeks."

"I wonder what the General will do next? He must have gone to immense time and expense building that staging area on Exoplanet W."

"I'm sure he did. It's a sure sign he's getting more capable and sophisticated. We're still ahead of him technologically and I'm pretty sure we have far more money but we haven't invested in weapons. Octavius won't hear of it. Depending how we deal with the General, that could be a serious disadvantage. We need to get the world's governments stirring and taking him on. Most of his activities so far have been off planet and clandestine. That needs to be exposed."

"Meanwhile, he took quite a hit. I hope you slowed him down. He must be furious."

"Let's hope so. What about this Moriarty?"

"He's next."

Chapter Nine

One of the cloned sheep waitresses *(not sure which one)* was serving drinks and nibbles. She had been listening to the conversation and couldn't wait to get back to the kitchens and tell them about the beautiful H.sap woman who was with the Bearoness and her mate. Where did she come from? She had a little white dog with her. Funny little thing. Didn't talk but danced up a storm.

Fiona, Directress of Lion and Unicorn Properties and Ventures, who had come up from the village and the offices, was taken aback with the appearance of Lady Juliet and her talented dog. "Och, a pair of beautiful haunts, are ye? I'm used to dealing with spirits, the liquid kind. I used to manage the Lounge here at the castle. Never met real ghosts before. And one is a doggie. Just like me. I'm a Dandie Dinmont. See my topknot! Oh, wait till Lion and Unicorn hear about this. They'll want you to make appearances at their pub and inns. Will you do that?"

Chita urged them on. "Go on Juliet. The locals and tourists will go wild."

The Baroness demurred. "Sorry, ladies. I'm here on a heavenly mission. I don't think my celestial superiors will think too highly of Pookie and I entertaining any more folks. We've already been over-exposed on American television. Especially the dog. Thanks for the opportunity but no. We won't be here long. Next stop is London after we confer on our problem."

"O dear, tis a shame. But I guess there's enough entertainment and excitement here to keep the guests happy. Lion and Unicorn have been doing their fighting routine more often than they used to. The tourists love it. Especially with a real live unicorn."

Juliet was not going to tell her that she had a ghost unicorn in her stables in Heaven. "Oh, here's the Bearoness. Hello again, Belinda. Looks like you have a full house."

"Juliet, Hello! Welcome! You too, Pookie. *(The dog jumped up and bowed to the Polar sow.)* Actually, two full houses! One group leaving on the ship and another on their way in to take their places. This cruise franchise is working out amazingly. Perhaps too much! But let's get on to the 'affaire du jour.'"

Fiona and the waitress left the rooms. The Colonel commented. "Well, the Baroness and her dog are back. That means we have more work to do with those two outlaws. You went back to Heaven for more guidance, didn't you? What do the celestial authorities have to say?"

"They want the two of them to be permanently thwarted but not executed. They want to extend mercy to those villains even though they don't have a merciful bone in either of their bodies."

"Ouch, did you try to reason with them?"

"With the Mother of God, compassion rules."

"Suppose we decide to ignore her wishes?"

Octavius snorted, "We will do no such thing, Colonel. Heaven has given us this assignment and we will follow it as required. As I understand it, Lady Juliet. Your next appointment is with Sherlock Holmes to plan how to deal with the Professor."

"Correct!"

"You should know I received a threatening interplanetary email from Moriarty insisting I desist in this campaign or suffer the consequences."

Juliet, never shocked, was indeed shocked. "You? How does Moriarty know about you?"

"No doubt from the General! I strongly resent being menaced, especially when my family and friends are included. By all means, contact Holmes and let him know about us and our destruction of the General's war machine."

"I don't think Holmes knows about you. Nor is he aware of the General and his plot. He also believes Moriarty is dead."

"Then we have to enlighten the Great Detective. Do you wish to take advantage of your relationship with him before I and the Octavians intervene? Enlighten him and tell him to expect to hear from me."

Belinda smiled, "But first, since you've materialized, let me show the two of you around Polar Paradise and invite you to enjoy drinks and one of Mrs. McRadish's gourmet dinners."

Juliet laughed, 'I think it would be better if I took our tour in our amorphous state. We don't want your guests wondering where an H. sap came from. Pookie can stay solid. A little white dog will fit right in as long as she behaves herself."

The Bichon was quite insulted to think she would be unruly and let the Baroness know with a series of outraged barks. Juliet ruffled her fur and said, "I'm sorry, dear. You are always a model of well-bred behavior." She reached into her reticule and pulled out a Heavenly Chewy to assuage the dog's pout. "OK, let's take a tour of Polar Paradise. I'm sure it has many characteristics of our celestial home."

Belinda felt a peculiar mental itch. She had the momentary inkling of having been to the Baroness' heavenly home. The image passed as rapidly as it came. What a ridiculous idea! Couldn't have happened! But for some reason, she thought of Heaven more frequently than she used to. She wondered why. Maybe it was just from meeting Juliet and Pookie. Yes, that must be it.

Maury had been quietly observing this by-play. Lately, he'd had an occasional image of Heaven, his dead sister and Mom and Dad. Just a dream or a daydream. Memory plays tricks. He still was having trouble figuring this celestial noblewoman out. She seemed real enough but ghosts still seemed unlikely to him. Oh, well. The Octavians dealt with a lot of unlikely things like Multi-Universe travel and Alternate Worlds; Ursulas; zapping Otters; crashing buildings and weapons into stars.

Octavius had no such problems. Supreme pragmatist that he is, his motto was the time worn, "it is what it is." The Baroness is here with an assignment and that's all there is to it.

"OK, One quick tour coming up and then down to business."

They started with a view from the balconies of the Bearonial Suite. Below, at the Cruise Terminal, the **North Wind** was preparing to cast off and continue its run to Scandinavia. The ship would return in a week and the mad exchange of tourists entering and leaving the resort would be replayed. Further down the beach, Harold, the Sea Otter was preparing the ski-doos, scuba diving, snorkeling and underwater gear along with kayaks, surfboards and other recreational craft for the new arrivals and directing the hotel staff in provisioning the yacht that would take today's party deep sea fishing. Pookie had wiggled her nose through the balcony bars and was enthralled by the action far below.

Juliet turned to Octavius and Belinda and said, "You certainly take advantage of the water here."

Belinda laughed, "Oh yes. Many of our visitors are aquatic or semi-aquatic and we provide them with a wide range of choices. The kids just love it. But we have a load of land based features. A carousel for the little ones, a nine hole golf course down at the village. Hiking and picnicking. And of course we have a number of entertainment venues here in the castle. The Aquabears still swim in our large aqua theater. I don't perform with them any more but as you know, I was once a famous aqueuse, Swimming, diving, dancing, Time moves on."

Octavius interrupted. "You've seen our lounges and the lobby. I'll take the two of you through the kitchens and then we'll go down to the sub-basements where all the scientific and techie staff is. Howard and Marlin's domain. It's a copy of the installation back in Cincinnati at the Bear's Lair. We can Quantum Travel from either location.

Mrs. McRadish was taken up with supervising dinner preparations and at first didn't notice the mortal and immortal entourage moving through her domain. She looked up, seeing only Maury and Octavius. Pookie had reluctantly desolidified in spite of all the delicious smells and the Baroness, an H.sap, didn't want to create a scene among the animal cook staff. "Och, Doctor Bear. Welcome to the kitchens and sculleries. We don't see you often. Your bairns, on the other paw, are in here constantly looking for snacks. They're little, nae, not so little, eating machines. Is there something I can fetch for you two."

"No thanks, Mrs. Mac. Just passing through. Everything smells terrific."

Juliet was impressed. Like the Twins and Pookie she enjoyed eating. They moved down to the next level where the Multiverse Lab and other technology rooms were located.

Octavius said, "You've been here before. I suggest we bring Sherlock Holmes here to convince him Earth Alpha and Polar Paradise exists and Moriarty is still alive.

Lady Juliet agreed. "But let me soften him up first."

*****

It took the Baroness practically no time to transit from Earth Alpha 2040 to Earth Beta London 1903. Pookie and the omnipresent Orifiel were with her. Holmes was still at Baker Street but was preparing to retire to Sussex. He was having no more success in his attempt than Octavius and Belinda were having with theirs.

London was its rainy, foggy self when the three of them descended on 221B, where Holmes kept his rooms. Watson lived with his wife and maintained his surgery in Queen Anne Street but was known to visit the genius detective often, especially when "the game was afoot." Such was the case when the celestial trio flitted up the seventeen stairs to the apartment and appeared. Orifiel stayed invisible. Mrs. Hudson was just clearing the morning's breakfast detritus, 'tsking' yet again at the deplorable state of the rooms and furniture. "Really, Mr. Holmes, do you intend to keep up your noxious experiments when you retire to East Dean?"

"Of course, dear lady. Between my bees, my writing and my experiments, I expect to live out the very fruitful remainder of my life as a Consulting Detective Emeritus. My young associate, Doctor Watson here has a full professional and personal life to keep him busy."

Juliet chose that moment to appear, with Pookie scampering over to the landlady. "Really, Holmes? A Consulting Detective Emeritus? How long will it take you to become totally and truly bored with your pastoral existence?"

"Ah, Baroness and Pookie. How nice to see you again. Welcome back! How go events in the celestial climes?"

"I'm not sure. I haven't spent much time in Heaven recently?"

Martha Hudson reacted, "Oh. goodness you haven't been expelled, have you?"

Juliet giggled, "No, dear! Pookie and I are still saintly citizens in good standing. I have been engaged in a rather complex endeavor. It seems…"

Holmes interrupted, "A complex endeavor in which you wish to get Watson and myself involved!"

"Well yes, Mr. Smart Boots. As usual you've gotten it in one."

"The answer is 'No!'"

"You haven't even heard my request!"

"And I don't want to. I am about to retire and I have no desire to be chasing off after another heaven inspired undertaking or more likely, a debacle inspired by you, my quite junior former partner. I'm sure Watson feels the same, engaged as he is with his marriage and medical practice."

The Doctor coughed, "Let me speak for myself, Holmes. I for one, would like to hear the Baroness out.'

"Thank you, Doctor. I'll tell you and Martha about the situation. Mr. Hostility Holmes can read his paper or pack his bags or whatever."

The detective snorted and picked up The Times, rattling the sheets as he did.

Juliet soldiered on. "First off, there are other worlds in our universe."

Holmes grunted. Watson and Mrs. Hudson looked at her with interest. "Martha said, "Of course, dear. There's Heaven. That's where you come from and that terrible place, Hell. Is there a Purgatory?"

"There is but that's not what I'm talking about. As a man of science, Doctor, I'm sure you are aware that we live on Planet Earth, Earth Beta to be exact, amid a cluster of other planets that orbit our Sun. Our detective friend has no interest in such cosmic trivia."

"Earth Beta?"

"Exactly! Beyond our solar system, there are a myriad of stars, some of which have planets, that is exoplanets, rotating about them. One of those planets millions of miles and years away, is Earth Alpha. It's populated by animals. Homo sapiens once lived there but a solar disaster did them in. The animals took over, prospered and now lead a civilization far more advanced than ours."

Holmes, pretending not to listen, expostulated, "Sheer utopian twaddle! Old wives' tales."

She retorted, "I've been there. Their technology would beggar your capabilities. They are at least 125 years ahead of this world in some respects. High speed aircraft, super-fast computing machines, long distance communications, scientific breakthroughs. They have a highly intelligent device called an Ursula that you, Holmes should become aware of. They are also socially advanced. You'd be pleased to know how much women have prospered, Martha, to the extent that some lead their countries. And their medical progress is remarkable, Doctor. You'd be amazed. But in one respect, Earths Alpha and Beta are the same. Evil! Satan does his work there as well as here and other planets. Crime, mayhem, dictators, suppression, starvation, mad men and women.

Holmes chuckled disparagingly. "Well at least, detectives must still be busy in this dream world."

"They are. I've met a few. One is eager to meet you. His name is Octavius Bear. A brilliant Kodiak polymath. He and his wife, oddly enough a Bearoness, are fabulously wealthy, have two marvelous estates and a team of highly talented associates, twin children and a technological empire, you wouldn't believe. They call themselves the Octavians."

Holmes said, "You're right. I don't believe."

Mrs. Hudson stared at him fiercely. She had been petting Pookie but listening, fascinated. "Mr. Holmes, do you realize you are calling a saint a liar? For shame!"

"Thank you, Martha. Right now, Octavius is engaged in a battle with a degenerate horse committed to cosmic conquest. His name is General Turmoil. He has been preparing equipment and forces to carry out subjugation of the universe. The Octavians destroyed his resources but the battle wages on."

Martha was amazed. Watson was perplexed. "Baroness. This is all quite fascinating and I do believe you but how does this involve us. As you say, this Earth Alpha is many millions of - what's the word?"

"Light years!"

"Yes, light years away and hundreds of years ahead of us in development and populated by highly cultivated and sentient animals. What possible impact can we have on this so-called battle?"

"I failed to mention this insane horse has an equally demented partner. Your old nemesis, Professor James Moriarty."

Holmes threw his paper on the floor. "Lady Juliet. I admit you cannot lie without bringing the fury of heaven on your head. But you are not omniscient and can be mistaken. We have seen that before. Let me state unequivocally, definitely and finally. Moriarty is dead. Period! Full stop!"

"And let me, dear former partner, state unequivocally and definitely, that in spite of your beliefs and assurances, the Professor is alive, active and through the horse's Multiverse travel capability, deeply involved in this plot to rule the universe. They both need to be stopped. Octavius is doing his part. You need to do yours."

"No, not without further proof. Moriarty is dead, I am retiring. Earth Alpha is a figment as is your magnificent Bear and his cohorts."

Juliet stamped her celestial foot. "I see you need more convincing. Well, you shall get it and not from me. Farewell Martha! Goodbye Doctor! It was wonderful to see you again. Come, Pookie. Don't get stung by your bees, Holmes."

Chapter Ten

(Earth Alpha – Polar Paradise – the Shetlands – 2030)

(Narrated by Maury Meerkat)

As you may also know, among his many talents and accomplishments, Octavius Bear is a brilliant, self-taught practitioner in the wide-ranging fields of biology, physics, ursinology, psychology, voodoo, teleology, chemistry, apiculture and oenology. He is a self-made gazillionaire and sole owner of UUI *(Universal Ursine Industries.)* He is also a first rate electrical, electronic, structural, marine, computer science, aeronautical, civil, mechanical and chemical engineer. The Great Bear has a few other interesting characteristics such as falling into brief, deep narcoleptic comas – side effects of his successful genetic experiments to eliminate the need for him to hibernate. However, the talent and occupation that has dominated his life is his avocation for criminology.

Lately, he has also turned his significant attentions to the existence, characteristics and accessibility of alternate universes. The Multiverse Project! Other worlds have figured mightily in many of the tales contained in *The Casebooks of Octavius Bear.* We have incontrovertible proof that other biospheres exist. Some are populated by intelligent beings. Some are not. We've been to many of these places and continue to journey to new as well as familiar sites.

Two of our Multiverse teammates, Hairy Otter *(aka Otto the Magnificent)* and Colonel Wyatt Where, a formidable wolf, have made most of the trips. Otto has a special talent for teleportation, allowing him to "zap" from place to place whenever his adrenaline is up to the task. The Colonel uses a more "conventional" mode of sleep-induced transit under the guidance of our Chief Scientist, Howard Watt Ph.D., a porcupine. Howard, along with his Dolphin associate Marlin, directs and implements our Multiverse program. All in all, we are awash in awe-inspiring intellects.

Little did we know we would shortly be in the presence of another awe-inspiring intellect: Sherlock Holmes.

*****

Lady Juliet Armstrong, Baroness Crestwood, late of Earth Beta, currently of the Heavenly Kingdom, her dog Pookie and her omnipresent angel assistant Orifiel flitted invisibly into the lounge of Polar Paradise. Clearly, she was in an unsaintly snit.

She appeared to me. "Maury, I need to talk with Octavius and Belinda. Where are they?"

"The Bearoness is in her office and Octavius is down in the Multiverse Lab with Howard, Wyatt, Otto and Marlin. They're trying to improve the rough landing sequence of the Quantum Travel unit. Something with your flitting you need not be concerned about."

"Well, I do have something or someone I'm deeply concerned about. Sherlock Holmes! He's being his obstreperous self. I need help from the Octavians to convince him that Earth Alpha exists and Professor Moriarty is still alive."

"You go down to the Lab! I'll stop off and see if Belinda is available."

I headed for the Bearoness' office. She was checking up on the recent passenger transfers to and from the **North Wind**. "Hello, Maury. It seems our relationship with the Solar Seas Cruise Company is paying off quite nicely. I'm thinking of setting up tour packages with the airlines. Fly into Abeardeen and then transfer by helicopter to Polar Paradise. What do you think?'

"Sounds good if you can get the right rates and discounts. Soar Polar! Chita would love it. She hates flying but would have a ball working up the publicity and marketing. She's doing a great job with the cruise ship."

"What a talent she is! What can I do for you?"

"Lady Juliet is back. It seems she's met some resistance from Sherlock Holmes. He doesn't believe Earth Alpha or we exist and is certain that Moriarty is dead."

"Well, I think we can do something about that. We have to end this horrible menace those two maniacs represent. Holmes is the best one to deal with the Professor although Octavius is enraged by the email he sent threatening us all. Where is Juliet now?"

"I left her flitting down to the Multiverse Lab. Howard, Marlin, Wyatt, Otto and Octavius are there working out some bugs in the Quantum unit. Of course, so are a couple of Ursulas who are hooked up with Condo back at the Kentucky Hexagon."

"These manifests can wait. Let's go to the Lab."

She and I headed for the elevators. Meanwhile Juliet and Pookie had arrived at the Lab and had manifested themselves. I understand an angel accompanies them but never appears. Octavius and Otto saw them first. Howard, Wyatt and Marlin were running tests on the equipment. In addition to softening the landings, they were raising the power to move larger objects further and faster. Who knew what weapons the Terrible Two would come up with next?

Otto squeaked, "Baroness, welcome back. Always a pleasure to see you and Pookie." The dog was sniffing at the large Transit Loop and doing somersaults through it.

"Pookie, come away from that. I don't want to chase after you through outer space."

The Bichon whined but crawled under one of the consoles and pouted.

Octavius had been listening to this and said, "I think we may have a way of dealing with the wily professor. Maybe the horse as well. Greetings, Baroness. How did it go with Holmes?'

"It didn't. That's why I'm back here. He insists Moriarty is dead. Also, for a constantly experimenting genius, he has a terrible blind spot when it comes to certain types of cosmic science. He can conjure up all sorts of chemicals and substances but the idea of alternate universes and specifically Earth Alpha just doesn't resonate with him."

"Well, we'll have to broaden his horizons. Suppose we invite him to visit Polar Paradise." Belinda and I had arrived. "What do you think, Bel? Maury?"

"I think we need to show him. Bring him here. *(She remembered Maury doubting Heaven existed but he couldn't recall how he, Octavius or she had been convinced. Funny how images of her mother, Beartha Black, kept popping up in her mind. She didn't realize the celestial memory blanking was still working.)*

Juliet looked dubious "I'm not sure he'll come."

"We can give him an assist. Howard, can we use the Quantum Travel system to reach back to Earth Beta London 1903?"

"A little time travel, huh? Yeah, I think we can especially with the enhancements we're installing. Give us a little more time to shake the techniques down. Who or what are we going to move."

"Sherlock Holmes for starters and then maybe other subjects and objects."

"Sherlock Homes, hmm! Always wanted to meet him. I wasn't sure he really existed."

"He feels the same about us. The Baroness has been in contact with him and he's resisting her efforts to get him to join our campaign against General Turmoil and Professor Moriarty. I want to bring him here."

"Why don't we give it a couple of tests. First, we'll send an Ursula and if she signs off, maybe Otto can take a trip. What do you think, my whiskered friend?"

"Time travel to London, Earth Beta in 1903 and meet Sherlock Holmes? Sounds like a fun adventure. Maybe Watson will be there, too."

Octavius turned to Juliet, "What is it Holmes always says. 'The sport is on the hoof'?"

Juliet laughed, "No, 'the game is afoot'. It's a speech of King Henry V in a play by Shakespeare. You call him Shakesbear. The game in question is animals. Sorry about that."

"Oh, well. Why don't you and Bel go and have a drink while you wait. Bring your dog. We don't want her flying around the universe by accident. She seems enthralled by the Quantum Transit systems."

"Oh, yes! Typical Pookie! Inquisitive to a fault. No! 'Nosey' is the better word. But then so am I. We spirits move around the Cosmos with ease. The whole idea of mortals being able to flit or zap from planet to planet, galaxy to galaxy, multiverse to multiverse was beyond my imagination. But you convinced me. Now, can we convince Sherlock Holmes? Brilliant man but unwilling to change his viewpoints easily. It took me quite a while to convince him I was a real immortal. He's still uncomfortable with the concept and the reality."

Octavius grinned. "Funny you should mention that. One minute I was all disbelief but suddenly I was more than wiling to accept what you were telling us. Quite convincing, Baroness."

Juliet smiled. Little did the Great Bear know. The celestial memory wipe is quite effective. All recollection of events gone but belief is enhanced.

Convincing Holmes is going to take something different. Hopefully Otto and Octavius will be able to pull it off. They're an amazing pair.

Chapter Eleven

(Earth Beta – Great Britain – London – 221B Baker Street – 1903)

(Narrated by Doctor John H. Watson)

"I see one of your literary competitors has turned from scientific scholarship to fictional musings, Watson. H.G. Wells has just published an imaginative adventure called the Time Machine. Travel through Time! Off to the Future. Back to the Past. Amusing ideas but sheer poppycock!"

"Oh, I don't know, Holmes. 'There are more things in heaven and earth, Horatio, than are dreamt of in your philosophy.' Are there no more marvels to be invented? Are we at the end of our world's development? As a doctor and scientist, I sincerely hope not."

"As a committed pragmatist and researcher, I await many new inventions but not those that defy the laws of nature. Time is irreversible. It flows in one direction at a fixed pace and cannot be accelerated. Visitations from the past or the future are impossible. We may be able speed up mechanical processes. The horseless carriage shows great promise. The Time Machine does not."

I shrugged my shoulders. I enjoy fantasy. Clearly Holmes doesn't. I idolize Jules Verne. Underwater travel; powered flight; circumnavigating the Earth; voyages to the Poles; fantastic islands. As I stood reflecting, I noticed out of the corner of my eye, a small figure who was not there a moment ago. It was a hairy animal no bigger than a footstool wearing a backpack. It was standing by a table. I reached for my cane to shoo it away when it spoke.

"Excuse me, gentlemen. Which of you is Mister Sherlock Holmes?"

I stood dumbstruck. Holmes navigated his head around the newspaper he had been reading and gaped at our small visitor. "Who…what do you want…how did you…? I'm speaking to a small animal as if it could talk and understand me."

"Oh, but I can. Please, Doctor Watson. I assume you are he. Put down that weapon."

A second later he appeared on top of a bookshelf and stared at me. Holmes continued to gape. "How did you do that? Who or what are you?"

"As you often say, Mr. Holmes. 'All will be revealed in good time.' My name is Hairy Otter or Sir Otto the Magnificent, Otto for short. I am from a different universe and time. I am here to seek your help with a problem which will soon be afflicting both our worlds. I think you will find it interesting."

Chapter Twelve

(Earth Alpha – Shetlands – Polar Paradise – 2030)

(Narrated by Maury Meerkat)

The Great Bear took up his oversize smart phone and pushed a button. "Howard? Octavius! Is he there yet?"

"He just arrived. And he has an Ursula with him. I'm still amazed that she can operate in alternate universes. I have Colonel Where on standby in case things don't work out. Of course, Otto can just 'zap' out of there if he needs to, but I think our little diplomat is quite capable of taking care of himself and completing the mission. He's done it several times before."

"I know. He looks like such a goof and often acts it, but I trust him to do an effective job. We need to deal with this threat in both venues."

I asked, "How did we get mixed up with this? Was it the Baroness and her heavenly mission?"

"Primarily! But as I told you at the meeting, Maury, we've been keeping an eye on Earth Beta for quite a while. They're 125 years behind us in development but our history and theirs seems to match up very closely. Their science and technology is advancing. We've been able to predict events in their universe by simply superimposing our own experiences on them. For example, useful air transportation is in their offing. Electricity is spreading rapidly. Telegraphy is becoming a mature communications system. The telephone is developing. Steam powered, electrical and internal combustion vehicles are on the drawing boards and on the roads. The Industrial Revolution is in full swing on Earth Beta."

"Society is changing as well but some things remain the same. Women have more rights. The class system is slowly dissolving. But, as we know, the criminal element is still in full force and growing more and more sophisticated. They too, are adapting to new scientific, industrial and societal tools and techniques. They cannot imagine the Internet and Social Media as sources for crime, but that time will come as computing and telecommunications explode. We have pledged not to interfere with their world's development, but we have a need for self-defense and we will limit our intervention to a very few people like Sherlock Holmes and Doctor Watson."

Howard spoke up, "Watson is an author. How are you going to keep him from broadcasting all he learns in this exercise?"

"We'll treat him the same way H.G. Wells and Jules Verne are being treated. As speculative fantasists. Entertaining, provocative but not to be taken seriously by the good citizens of Earth Beta 1903."

"Why are you pursuing Sherlock Holmes and Doctor Watson on Earth Beta? I thought we were avoiding biospheres in which 'Homo Sapiens' still exists."

"Because one 'Homo Sapiens' who is supposed to be dead, still exists."

"Sorry, that went over my head."

"Maury, you know the General but are you familiar with Professor James Moriarty?"

"Can't say that I am."

"Holmes refers to him as the Napoleon of Crime. He was supposed to have succumbed from a fall off Reichenbach Falls in Earth Beta Switzerland while battling Holmes. He didn't."

"How do you know?"

"Because he's here."

"A 'Homo Sapiens' is here? He'd stick out like the proverbial sore paw on an all-animal planet."

"Most would. Not him. Like Sherlock Holmes, he's a master of hiding and disguise."

"He's from Earth Beta. What does he want with our world?"

"To control it and repopulate it with 'H. Saps' of his own choosing. Needless to say, they would all be beholden and subordinate to the Napoleon of Crime. Think what he could do with our technology, weaponry and social structures. It would mean the eventual end of our society."

"How did he get here?"

"I'm not sure, but I strongly suspect some animal from The Business, perhaps General Turmoil himself, may have fallen for his act and made their experiments in multiverse travel available to him in exchange for a major position in his new empire."

(General Turmoil is a Horse who heads up a U.S. Federal Government sponsored, semi-military, semi-spy organization called The Business. He has also been actively pursuing alternative universes with conquest in mind. Octavius has been at odds with him for a long time and Colonel Where, while

he was still in the Army, ended up as an experimental subject of the General's. All told, a nasty equine piece of work.)

"If you know he's here, why don't we just capture him and throw him over another waterfall?"

"He's too clever for that. That's why I want Sherlock Holmes' assistance. I wonder how Otto is doing?"

Chapter Thirteen

(Earth Beta – Great Britain – London – 221B Baker Street – 1903)

(Narrated by Doctor John H. Watson)

Eventually Holmes and I stopped staring at this Otto creature and summoned enough presence of mind to agree that this was not a joint figment of our imagination.

"Clearly, you are here and neither of us seems to be hallucinating so let us deal with the evidence before us." said Holmes. "I am indeed Sherlock Holmes, and this is my associate, Doctor John H. Watson. You obviously know who we are and have somehow managed to enter our rooms undetected. You seem to possess the ability to, what is the word, 'teleport.' I assume our landlady, Mrs. Hudson is not aware of you. You are an intelligent and verbally capable member of the mammalian species Mustelidae Lutrinae. You say you are here from another sphere and time to seek our help with an interesting problem which will soon be afflicting both our worlds. May I tell you, Mister Otto, that you strain credulity. I believe that you are a superbly trained and possibly biologically altered music hall trickster."

The otter smiled. "You don't know how very close to the truth you are, Mr. Holmes. Your powers of observation are quite keen. However, let me demonstrate that I am not from your place or time."

He took off his backpack and pulled out what looked like a glass covered slate. He laid it on the table in front of us. "Allow me to introduce my associate, Ursula."

A cat-like face appeared on the surface of the slate. A female voice emanated from it.

"Thank you, Otto! Hello, Mr. Holmes and Doctor Watson. I am an Artificial General Intelligence System. My official nomenclature is Universal Ursine Intellect Model 18 – Ursula 18 for short. My origins date back to Charles Bearbage's efforts to create an Analytical Engine or as we now call it, a mechanical computer. You may also be familiar with the work of Ada Airedale, Countess of Lovelace, in developing procedures for the machine or in our terminology, programs.

In our time, their first efforts progressed to the creation of the electronic computer, a term I'm sure is not familiar to you. However, it will eventually revolutionize your civilization. My most recent predecessor systems were developed by the Advanced Super Computing Center at Doctor Octavius Bear's Universal Ursine Industries (UUI.) The Computing Center team and I used those earlier versions to create a further enhanced entity - me, the Model 18. We are working together on a Model 19 which in turn will help produce even more sophisticated and powerful Artificial Intelligence systems. Each advanced unit contains the capabilities, memories and power of its progenitors so, in a sense, we are not replacing but rather expanding the Ursula family.

While I am physically supported by a highly secure and hyper-powered server farm back in the American state of Kentucky on Earth Alpha, I also exist in clouds and network-based nodes and can be instantaneously incorporated into a wide variety of independent devices like this one. My extremely high-speed multi-tasking abilities allow me to continuously serve a very large number of entities while simultaneously and independently enhancing my own abilities. I have limitless Deep and Big Data access and analytical capabilities. Much of this is meaningless to you but it permits me to be of immense and immediate service to my associates."

"I can see, hear and feel. I now also have a sense of smell. Your shag tobacco is most redolent. I speak and understand an almost infinite number of languages and dialects. I can change my appearance and my vocal output to suit most moods and situations. Right now, I feel like being a Lynx. I can interact with other devices, vehicles and structures and of course, all varieties of sentient individuals in these worlds. I am an important component of Doctor Octavius Bear's Multiverse Project and am adapting my capabilities to deal with alternate universes such as your own as they are discovered. I have also been instrumental in bringing many criminals to book.

I have restraining functions which prevent me from doing deliberate harm even in self-defense, unless I am released by a recognized authority using very carefully protected clandestine codes. Finally, I have been told that although the Model 18 is shy on emotions, I have developed a finely-honed sense of humor."

"I and my associate, Sir Otto the Magnificent are here to convince you that Earth Alpha and the Octavians exist. Our assignment is to get you to believe that Professor Moriarty still lives as Baroness Juliet tried to tell you. He and the rogue General Turmoil have major ambitions of conquering the Cosmos. That must certainly be consistent with the Professor Moriarty you tangled with in the past. Have no doubt. The professor will be targeting you shortly. He and the General will not allow you to stand in their way. Believe Lady Juliet and let us help you"

The silence descended on us like a shroud. This was a development that needed careful analysis.

Holmes finished filling his pipe and I took the time to further examine first this miraculous device and then the otter. "Are you unique or is there an entire species like you?"

"I am a river otter. My family comes from the St. Lawrence Valley in Earth Alpha Canada. You should know that your species, Homo Sapiens, was destroyed on our world in a global catastrophe over 100,000 years ago. However, many animals, birds and reptiles were positively affected by that same catastrophe and took on major anthropomorphic characteristics. We are much like you or you are much like us. My ability to teleport is unique to me, as far as I know, and as Mr. Holmes surmised, was the result of biological alteration which was unwillingly inflicted on me by a villain named Imperius Drake. He is now dead but was very much like your Professor Moriarty, the reason I am here."

Holmes persisted. "Moriarty is also dead."

"I'm afraid not, Mr. Holmes. He's alive and well and threatening our worlds. He wants to restore Homo Sapiens to Earths Alpha and Beta but on his terms. You have referred to him as the Napoleon of Crime in your writings. He wishes to become the Emperor of our Cosmos."

"How do you know all this?"

"Simple, he told us, or more exactly he told Octavius Bear in a menacing letter."

"Just who is this Doctor Octavius Bear?" I asked.

Otto took a deep breath and rattled off a description of this ursine paragon. His size; his brainpower; his inventive skills; his dedication to righting wrongs; his partnership with law enforcement; his list of overpowered criminals; his wealth; his fame; his associates; his family including his Bearoness wife and their twin cubs living in the Earth Alpha Shetland Islands and Cincinnati. He concluded with, "You should be meeting him shortly. I'm here to arrange a collaboration to rout Professor Moriarty from both our worlds. We have already temporarily disarmed his associate, General Turmoil but he is still at large. I hope you will agree to cooperate with us in defeating Moriarty No one knows him better and your knowledge and mutual support will be invaluable."

Holmes paused, looked at the ceiling and said, "I suppose I could say that he is your problem. As far as this world is concerned, he is dead."

"No, he's not. Just remember, Mr. Holmes, that he can traverse the Multiverse. If I could get here, so can he. Also remember that there is no one Moriarty hates more than you."

"Your point is well made, Mr. Otto. All right, let us meet with Doctor Bear. May I suggest we do so at a location far from London. If Moriarty is indeed alive and active, he will have spies and operatives active as well. Watson, we may even now be under his surveillance. We must take care. There is nothing so deadly as overconfidence. Mr. Otto, how shall we communicate with you?"

"I'll leave this duplicate of the Ursula system with you for the time being. At any given moment there are a large number of Ursula AGI copies functioning. I warn you. She is quite independent and slavishly faithful to the Great Bear. Any attempt to misuse or exploit her abilities will be met with severe resistance. Don't try to deconstruct the device. If you try to show her or demonstrate her to others it will result in a self-destruct. Don't underestimate her. She is quite powerful."

A chime rang out from the laptop. "Thank you, Otto. I am here to help, Mr. Holmes and Doctor. My unit's power is supplied by the sun. I can communicate over the Multiverse. May I also offer you suggestions from time to time? Where do you think this meeting should be held?"

Holmes looked at me. "Scotland?"

I agreed. "What do you think, Otto?" He had disappeared. I turned to Holmes. "Please don't say 'The game is afoot.' I shall look at the Bradshaw and find an appropriate train."

The Ursula device chimed again. "There's no need, Doctor Watson. I have booked the two of you in separate compartments on tomorrow morning's express to Edinburgh. May I suggest you then proceed to St. Andrews in Fife. I have made reservations at the Redbryers outside of town. You may also wish to arrive at the station separately. Since you will be gone for three days, you might want to concoct some story to satisfy Mrs. Hudson's curiosity."

Holmes shook his head in disbelief. "Thank you, Miss Ursula!"

She replied, "I shall remain with you and facilitate the meeting between you and Doctor Bear. When you decide on your action plan against the Professor, I will help to carry it out. I suggest exile for him on an unpopulated exoplanet."

Holmes was still having trouble getting his mind and emotions around the Multiverse concept. Watson asked, "Why not just kill him?"

"That would seem to be the simplest solution but the Queen of Heaven to whom the Baroness reports has insisted that no or very few lives be taken in this conflict."

"The Queen of Heaven is involved?"

"It is at her command that we are carrying out this mission."

"Even though, if you are to be believed, Moriarty and this General would not hesitate to wipe out entire civilizations?"

"The Queen and her Son are highly benevolent. Compassion is very powerful, Doctor. As a physician, I'm sure you know that."

I sat and pondered.

Chapter Fourteen

(Earth Alpha – the Shetlands – Polar Paradise- 2030)

(Narrated by Maury Meerkat)

"Maury, Is Otto back yet?" Octavius' roar rang through the Bearonial Suite.

"He just arrived. Howard is checking him out."

"Well, tell him I want to see him as soon as he's ready. Meanwhile, call up Ursula."

The AGI chimed from a large laptop sitting on the Bear's desk. "Yes, Doctor Bear, I'm here. I am also currently with Mr. Holmes and Doctor Watson. They have agreed to take up the Moriarty issue. They are leaving on holiday for St. Andrews, Scotland tomorrow morning. It's a famous golf resort far from London. They thought it would be remote enough not to bring on any suspicion by the Professor's minions. Watson plays golf. Holmes, as you might suspect, does not. You should be able to meet with them day after tomorrow."

"Meanwhile, I have located Professor Moriarty here on Earth Alpha. He is squirreled away in a Washington D.C. suburb not far from the offices of the Business. My Deep Data algorithms conclude with 96% certainty that General Turmoil is providing the professor with the means to transit back and forth between the two Earths. He has made the trip several times. General Turmoil, has his hooves deeply in this plan to conquer the Cosmos. Here is Otto."

The otter entered Octavius' office munching on a fish and holding a bowl of fermented kelp juice. "Good evening, Octavius. Multiverse travel creates a real appetite. Mission accomplished, as Ursula probably told you."

"Yes, she did. Well done! Now, I want you, Belinda, Maury, Howard, Marlin, the Colonel, Frau Schuylkill, Senhor Condor and I to strategize our approach to dealing with the Professor. I want to present a logical plan to Holmes and Watson that will ensure their cooperation. First off, Maury, have we received any more correspondence from Moriarty?"

"No, only that first letter threatening to demolish you, your family, associates and empire."

"He certainly thinks in imposing terms. Reminds me somewhat of Imperius Drake. *(See The Casebooks of Octavius Bear-Book 1-The Open and Shut Case.)* I'm pretty certain we have General Turmoil to thank for Moriarty's attention. I am just about positive The Business is serving as his Alternate Universe Transit System. I wonder how the two of them got together. I can see where their mad dreams of multiverse conquest would coincide. That horse is mad."

"Perhaps Sherlock Holmes can shed some more light on it."

Chapter Fifteen

(Earth Beta – Great Britain – Scotland – St. Andrews – 1903)

(Narrated by Doctor John H. Watson)

We traveled in separate cabins by first class rail to Edinburgh, then on another train over the spectacular Forth Bridge and finally by coach to St. Andrews. We believe we evaded any detection that the Professor may have set upon us. My body was stiff from the trip and I was looking forward to playing a round of golf to loosen up my tightened muscles. Not so, Holmes. He was in continuous contact with the Ursula Artificial General Intelligence unit, trying to gain a greater insight into how this marvel from the future worked and what general knowledge about it he could glean. Unfortunately, whenever the conversation turned to matters of scientific development supporting this device, Ursula skillfully turned back his advances. I think I heard him mutter, "She is more elusive than Irene Adler."

Holmes is convinced the AGI is a real human person with greatly enhanced capabilities supported by advanced communications functions. Several times, in frustration, I believe he came close to smashing the device. She continues to amaze. I found myself with a greens reservation and rented golf clubs to play the course with several local medical practitioners. Courtesy of Ursula. We had a delicious meal at a local inn suggested by our constant companion.

Finally, late in the evening of our second day in Scotland, she rang her chime which was rapidly becoming a source of irritation for Holmes.

"Mr. Holmes, Doctor Watson! Doctor Octavius Bear will be joining you at ten o'clock tomorrow morning at your rooms at the Inn. He would appreciate a briefing on Professor Moriarty including all of your experiences with him and insights about him. The Professor has blatantly threatened him, his family, his associates and Universal Ursine Industries with total destruction. Obviously, this does not sit well with the genius we refer to as the Great Bear. He wishes to join forces with you in essentially eliminating Moriarty and his associate, General Turmoil. The Professor is obviously a major threat in both of your worlds as well as the entire universe. Can you confirm your availability and willingness?"

Holmes and I looked at each other. He spoke. "We will cooperate, but we will need to have several questions answered which you, my mysterious friend, have shown yourself unwilling to address."

The AGI replied. "I am not authorized to speak for him, but I am sure both sides will reach agreement and act accordingly. My statistical algorithms predict success."

What in the name of all that is holy are 'statistical algorithms'?

*****

At precisely ten o'clock, we sat in our room, finishing off cups of Scottish coffee when a loud thump brought us both to our feet. A huge, brown, fur-covered object landed dangerously close to our chairs. An oversize head emerged and loudly yawned, baring an array of ominous looking teeth. It righted itself and momentarily stared at both of us while still seated on the floor.

Holmes smiled, "Doctor Bear, I presume!"

Another yawn and snort. "Yes, I apologize for my ungraceful entrance but unlike my Otter friend and others, I must be asleep in order to transit the Multiverse. Not sure why that is necessary, but it seems to expedite the process. I assume that you are Mr. Sherlock Holmes and Doctor Watson."

I replied, "We are. I'm a medical doctor. Do you require any assistance after your journey?"

"No thank you, I'm quite awake now. I see one of our AGI units is keeping you company. Hello Ursula!"

"Hello Doctor Bear. Welcome to Earth Beta – Scotland 1903."

"Thank you. Please notify Howard and Marlin that I arrived safely and efficiently. I assume you have been assisting our friends as necessary."

Before Ursula could respond, Holmes said, "Yes, she has been most helpful, but she is quite expert in maintaining secrecy. Your technology is quite safe with her. But before we begin, I must insist that we have a better understanding of this Multiverse phenomenon and our mutual roles in combatting Moriarty and this so-called General."

"A fair request. First of all, alternate worlds do exist. We have discovered a few of them but our Multiverse Project is getting better at it. All of the ones we have found exist outside Earth Alpha's solar system. Some are populated. Several are not. I know, if you believe any of this, you are probably assuming we live in the future of your own world, much like the speculations of your friend H.G. Wells. Not so! Earth Alpha and Earth Beta are two locations far distant from each other circumnavigating dissimilar stars at different parts of the universe. "

"Civilizations develop at separate paces and we are more advanced technologically and biologically than your world, although we lost Homo Sapiens over 100,000 years ago. Psychologically and morally, I'm not sure who has the advantage. We have criminals. We seem to exist in endless states of war. We have hunger, ignorance, inequality, prejudice and all the other things that infect civilizations. As do you."

"What is exceptional is how closely we correlate with each other's development. If we go back 125 years in our own Earth Alpha's history, it looks remarkably like your Earth Beta today. The major difference lies in the presence of Homo Sapiens in your world and the growth of the animal kingdom in ours. Of course, that constitutes an immense variance but the similarities between our two worlds far outweigh the differences."

"It is only recently that we developed techniques to seek out alternate worlds. We do not cover distance in the conventional sense. We can use quantum measures that I cannot share with you. We must be extremely careful not to unduly influence Earth Beta's natural development. Even counteracting Moriarty has complications. But he is a threat to both our biospheres and must be dealt with. That is why I'm here to seek your assistance."

I had sat listening to this huge animal explaining in American English, the nature of the universes in which we dwelt. Torn between wonder and disbelief, I looked over at Holmes who seemed to share my feelings.

"Forgive me, Doctor Bear, but my profession has required me to be extremely skeptical of any phenomenon that falls outside normal experience and logic. There are, no doubt, many wonders remaining to unfold but I am loath to accept them without unshakeable proof."

"I understand, Mr. Holmes. Will you allow me a small demonstration? It will involve yourself and I don't wish to threaten you or abuse your hospitality. I propose to send you briefly to Earth Alpha and return you to this spot. I don't think you will need to be asleep as I have to be."

I started to protest but Holmes intervened. "Calm yourself Watson. I have never passed up a significant challenge and this would seem to be one. Have at it, Doctor Bear."

"Thank you. Please call me Octavius. Doctor Watson, you will be our witness. Mr. Holmes will disappear before your eyes and return in a few minutes. Ursula, please alert Howard to transport Mr. Holmes to Polar Paradise and return him with a small token of our appreciation."

The AGI addressed the mysterious porcupine Howard and issued a series of numbers and directions that sounded like artillery guidance. I objected "I say, Octavius, you're not going to shoot him from some sort of gun, are you?"

"Fear not, Doctor Watson. There is no weaponry involved. He will simply vanish from his chair and return to the same spot unchanged. Are we ready, Ursula?"

"Yes, Doctor Bear. Ready, Mr. Holmes?"

Holmes nodded his head. He and his closing words disappeared with a whooshing sound.

Octavius said, "He is now in transit. Tell us when he arrives, Ursula!"

She replied, "We are tracking him. Just a few more moments."

I panicked, "Can he still breathe? Is he undergoing pain? Is he conscious?"

Ursula replied, "Yes, he can breathe. There is no pain. He is conscious and there has been no change in his physical or mental status. We use this technique on our own staff and we are very caring about their welfare. We have had no accidents with living creatures. He has arrived."

Octavius looked at me and said, "When Holmes returns, I would appreciate a thorough briefing on this Professor Moriarty. His personality, motivations, history, modes of operation, vulnerabilities. What is it that makes him so formidable? I strongly resent the strength and arrogance of his threats to me and mine. I assume he believes that Holmes and I stand in the way of his conquest of the universe."

I replied, "I have not actually met the man himself. That has been Holmes' 'privilege' but I have encountered several of his minions. Villains all! Moriarty is the consummate planner. Staying in the background but controlling the process in detail. He is normally quite elusive but this time he seems to be taking direct initiatives. I wonder why."

"I have a theory," said the Bear. "I think he wants to exclusively capture all the technology he can glean from our work. He has, no doubt, gotten some insights from General Turmoil but he too is very jealous of his knowledge base, expertise and results."

"Who is this General Turmoil?"

"General Turmoil is a Horse who heads up a U.S. Government sponsored, semi-military, semi-spy organization called The Business. He has been actively pursuing alternative universes for years. We have clashed a number of times. He has gone rogue. Unbeknownst to our government, he has set world conquest and now, cosmic conquest as his sole objective. I will spell it out further when Sherlock Holmes returns from his trip to my establishment on Earth Alpha."

"In the meantime," I said. "I assume you know that Holmes disappeared for several years after the Reichenbach incident leaving me and my readers to assume that he was lost in the falls. He only recently reappeared after travels, he tells me, in the mysterious Far East. I still don't know all of the story."

"Well," the Bear responded, "we do, since we've had the benefit of reading 'Watson's Works' that you haven't written yet. Don't worry. I won't spoil it for you."

'You know," I replied, "this is very much like Wells' prediction of time travel."

"That's why it's so important that when we finish this adventure, we leave no traces of our world's existence. If you wish to write speculative fiction, go right ahead. We can't stop you. The only tangible effect I intend to leave is the permanent absence of Professor James Moriarty and General

Turmoil and I am engaged in that activity only because they have threatened the universe and especially me in my world and time. If we could eliminate Moriarty in Earth Alpha-2030, we would do so but because of the alliance he has built with The General and his ability to move between the two universes, we have had to pursue him here as well as back on Earth Alpha. We don't know how he survived the fall at Reichenbach but he did. Do you know, Doctor?"

Watson replied, "Until you arrived, I didn't think he did survive. Neither did Holmes. Although there have been a number of carefully planned and executed criminal activities that seemed well beyond the skills of the rogues who executed them. A mastermind seems be at work. But Moriarty has always been skilled at disguises and misdirection. As I think about it, his signature could well be on many of the crimes."

Octavius nodded, "But I assume lately he has been preoccupied with conquering the universe. The Professor is a devil – an evil genius – extremely skilled in Satanic machinations. Let's hope we can put a stop to it. I assume you know about the Baroness mission from the heavenly Queen and her requirement that no one perishes, including the General and Professor. It makes our solutions more difficult.".""

"Early on, she attempted to persuade Holmes of her mission. He was having none of it. Perhaps when he returns he'll be more amenable. Where is he? It's been a long time."

Chapter Sixteen

(Earth Beta – Great Britain – Scotland – St. Andrews – 1903)

(Narrated by Doctor John H. Watson)

Fifteen minutes had elapsed, and my fears rose with each passing second. Had Holmes been trapped in a plot against him? Was this gigantic bear an agent of Moriarty? Had something gone wrong technically or was this whole thing a farcical stunt? I had packed my service revolver but how effective it would be against a 9-foot-tall Kodiak remained to be seen. Besides, I had to reach into my luggage to get it out. And would it bring my friend and colleague back? I practically screamed at the Ursula device, "Where is he?"

Another 'whoosh' and Holmes himself responded. "Right here, old man. Thanks for your concern."

"Good Lord, Holmes, I thought you had disappeared forever."

"No, but I suspect that is what Octavius has in mind for Professor Moriarty. Am I correct, Doctor Bear."

The Great Bear grinned, "That thought had crossed my mind. Well, Mr. Holmes, are you convinced we can transit universes?"

"Either that or you have concocted a magnificent piece of theater."

"They are not mutually exclusive. I see you are holding onto our little gift."

"Yes, in the very few minutes I sat in your laboratory surrounded by an array of technical but undefined machines, an absolutely beautiful grey she-wolf *(Frau Schuylkill)* approached me, bowed and handed me this keg of Earth

Alpha mead - vintage 2015. She was silent as were most of the others there – a porcupine; a handsome male red wolf; a beautiful polar bear; two juvenile bear cubs and a little white curly-haired dog. The cubs were chattering in typical youthful fashion. The Baroness was there with her dog. She waved but didn't speak to me. I suppose she felt quite justified. I owe her an apology. Your associate Otto winked at me. A very large condor was also watching from some sort of screen. The porcupine signaled me to regain my seat and said something to a dolphin contained in a large glass tank. They then proceeded to speak to a twin copy of this Ursula here, waved at me and sent me on my way."

"Well," said the Bear, "shall we enter into a partnership to defeat our mutual enemy or are you still unconvinced of our intent? By the way, I hope you like mead."

"I do. Bees are wonderful creatures. I have been known, as Watson is well aware, to take risks without total prior assurance. What say you, my friend. Shall we establish the Interplanetary Society for the Defeat of Professor James Moriarty?"

I reluctantly nodded. "I agree with the objective. I am still unsure of the means. Moriarty is a most formidable adversary."

Octavius nodded, "But not insuperable, Doctor Watson. We are not without resources. Gentlemen, please tell me all you know about this criminal mastermind. Oddly enough, in spite of his remarkable threats against me, I have never met the man and know practically nothing about him. Ursula, please record this discussion and add your knowledge, opinions, theories and surmises. In turn, I will provide you two gentlemen with what we know about

General Turmoil and his organization. Moriarty seems to have him in thrall. I strongly suspect that's the original source of the threats."

Holmes took a moment to perform maintenance on his briar pipe. When he was satisfied, he sat back and began a short biography of Moriarty. "He is indeed, a brilliant professor of mathematics. He has several learned works to his credit on the Binomial Theory and the Dynamics of an Asteroid. However, his supremely hostile, nay diabolical, personality forced him to leave academe under a major cloud."

"He had already embarked on a life of crime, but he accelerated it and took on a small army of felons to do his bidding. He has been characterized as a noxious spider, pulling strings in his web to produce heinous acts of corruption. Nothing is too wicked or difficult to discourage him. However, he seldom works directly. To my knowledge, there are no official police reports naming him although his fame and fortune are more than sufficient to satisfy a lesser villain."

"I have been, I believe, the sole beneficiary of his direct attacks. After informing me that he could no longer tolerate my interference in his enterprises, he followed me to Switzerland where at the Reichenbach Falls, we engaged in hand-to-hand combat. The stories had it that we both perished in a drop over the rushing water. You now know that reports of our mutual demise were inaccurate and greatly premature."

"His ambition has risen dramatically and I suppose being the Napoleon of Crime is no longer satisfying. As you have indicated, he now characterizes himself as the Emperor of the Cosmos. In order to secure this position, he feels he must eradicate me for good and now that he has discovered your alternate world, you must be eliminated as well."

Ursula rang her chime. "How familiar is he with Earth Alpha? After all, Mr. Holmes and Doctor Watson, you knew nothing of us until Otto made his appearance."

Octavius intervened. "I suspect we have General Turmoil to thank for that. While not up to the standards of Project Multiverse, he and The Business have shown some ability to traverse alternate worlds. It may have been by accident or a deliberate search that led him to Earth Beta and ultimately to the Professor."

"He shares Moriarty's ambitions of cosmic conquest. If what you have told us of Moriarty's personality is true, he has no desire to have a partner. Nor do I believe does the General. They will tolerate each other and work together until the time for a no doubt violent breakup seems appropriate. The General knows enough about us to fill in the blanks for Moriarty. Now, we too are a threat to his plans, so we must be eliminated. You believe Moriarty is ruthless enough to carry out that process."

"I believe his ego may be such that, contrary to his normal mode of operating by remote control, he will take on those assignments himself. You are a long-standing irritant, Mr. Holmes and he has already attempted once to personally end your life. I believe he will try again. As for me, I don't think he wants to give the General the advantage of having eradicated UUI, my family, friends and associates. As we say in the American West, I believe these will be mano-a-mano duels. Do you agree?"

Watson frowned. "It seems most probable to me."

Holmes thought for a moment. "The Professor prides himself on being unpredictable. While I also think your scenario is the most probable, I believe we must think more broadly on other ways he will choose to act. Now, Octavius, do you have any plans?"

"Yes, I do but I need to explore with my staff what the best alternatives are. They have significant experience with the General and I want to draw on it. I am going to return to Earth Alpha, but I will leave this Ursula unit with you as an assistant. Ursula, will you please send another unit here for Doctor Watson's use?"

"Certainly, Doctor Bear. Are you ready to traverse?"

"I am but I will be in almost constant contact with both of you gentlemen through the Ursulas. Is there anything else we need to discuss before I leave?"

"Do you know where Moriarty is at the moment?"

"We believe he is still in Washington, Earth Alpha, with the General. We have been tracking him steadily. If it looks like he will be returning to your world, we'll notify you immediately. Regardless, I would suggest you stay acutely alert. We don't know, or perhaps you do know, who may be working for him here."

"He has an extensive Rogues' Gallery. We know most of them and will be on the lookout for them. We return to London tomorrow. It will take us longer to get home than it will you."

The Bear chuckled and with another 'whoosh' disappeared. Right on his heels, a second Ursula device materialized. "Doctor Watson, I presume! I am the same Ursula. At this moment, I am working with a number of Doctor Bear's team members as well as you and Mr. Holmes. When you communicate with either of these devices, you are interacting with me as well as all other Ursula manifestations. Actually, I use, but am independent of, the units you hold in your hand. We hope that is convenient."

I stared, trying to absorb this concept and dropped the unit.

A tinkling giggle. "Don't worry. The Ursula laptop is practically indestructible unless I am called upon to trigger it to 'self-destruct' to protect secrecy. Neither the Professor nor the General are aware of my existence and we want to keep it that way. Please tuck the units away safely. They are expensive. Thank you! Back to London tomorrow after a substantial meal tonight? I will make reservations."

Chapter Seventeen

(Earth Alpha – The Shetlands – Polar Paradise – 2030) and

(Earth Beta – Great Britain – London – 221B Baker Street – 1903)

Maury here! Octavius is back at Polar Paradise in conference with his team. Holmes and Watson are making their way back to London and 221B Baker Street. The consensus in each world is that Professor Moriarty will soon personally stage his attacks on both venues. No one is sure of his priorities. While his approach to Octavius may be clinical and strategic, his passionate hatred of Holmes and desire for revenge is probably going to lead him to that target first. Conquering both will result in him having free rein to control the Cosmos as we currently understand it and then rid himself of his would-be partner, the General.

The combined resources of Howard Watt and Ursula 18 have detected his return to the more familiar surroundings of London on Earth Beta. We believe he availed himself of General Turmoil's technology to make the transition. He is being constantly tracked 24/7/365.

The Bear's team has set a trap in readiness for whichever venue he chooses. Holmes and Watson have been instructed in the role that will be played by the Ursula units in their possession. The instruction to the British players has been brief, but emphatic. ***Don't let the Ursula units out of your possession unless Moriarty demands one and then only surrender one. Do not attempt to disarm, kill or otherwise capture him.***

A similar rule has been established at the Bear's Lair and Polar Paradise. Now we wait. The Ursula units are relaying communications between sites. Nothing has been heard from the General's operations. He may be waiting for Moriarty to fail. An honorable partnership.

After a lengthy and not too comfortable trip back from St. Andrews, Holmes and Watson reached 221B and the enthusiastic ministrations of their landlady.

"Mrs. Hudson, what are you doing here?"

"What a wonderful greeting, Doctor!"

"It's just that…well, it's dangerous."

"Dangerous? In my own house?"

A new voice responded. "He is quite correct, Mrs. Hudson. You should not be here but it's too late for you to leave."

Moriarty emerged from Holmes' bedchamber with a revolver pointing in the direction of the woman. "Sherlock Holmes, I have borne indignities, interference and threats from you for far too long. No longer. The same applies to your idiot Boswell. There is no hope for the two of you, but I may choose to overlook your landlady, if you comply with my demands. I am, after all, not without chivalry."

Holmes looked directly at the Professor. "What do you want, Moriarty?"

"One of my functionaries who has been trailing you has noticed a peculiar device that seems to converse with you. I intend to examine and make use of that apparatus. I am not sure what functions it performs but I will shortly find out. I give you my word as a gentleman that no harm will come to this lady, if you agree to hand it over."

"Give it to him, Watson."

"But Holmes…"

"Give it to him, NOW!"

The doctor reluctantly reached into his bag as Mrs. Hudson cried out, "Doctor, don't do it! He's a scoundrel and will not live up to his promise."

The Professor smiled. "What difference does it make, Mrs. Hudson? I can receive it as a gift or take it from his dead hand. Either way I shall have it."

Holmes once again looked at Watson and said, "Do it NOW!"

Watson took the Ursula laptop out of his bag and handed it to Moriarty.

"Thank you! Don't expect to distract me. I can examine this at my leisure. Meantime…"

A whooshing sound and the Professor, his revolver and the Ursula device disappeared.

Mrs. Hudson screamed, "Where is he? Where did he go?"

Holmes smiled, "Never fear, Mrs. Hudson. He will not return."

The Ursula laptop in Sherlock Holmes' hand chimed. "I can report that the Professor has landed on Biosphere Y, a jungle-infested, unpopulated rock. He is alone with his pistol. General Turmoil does not have his coordinates and cannot come to his aid. I have triggered the laptop device in his possession to totally self-destruct. We don't want to leave any evidence of our presence or assist him in any way."

Another whoosh and Otto appeared, scaring the landlady but causing Holmes and Watson to break out in relieved laughter. Holmes smiled at the otter and said, "Mr. Otto. I presume you have come to retrieve your property. We greatly enjoyed having Ms. Ursula with us. Here she is. Thank Doctor Bear profusely for us and have a good quantum journey."

Chapter Eighteen

(Earth Alpha – The Shetlands – Polar Paradise – 2030)

Memo to: General Turmoil-The Business

From: Doctor Octavius Bear-UUI

Subject: Professor James Moriarty

We have been advised that your erstwhile colleague has disappeared and will probably remain in that status.

May I strongly suggest that you forthwith terminate your operations dealing with Earth Beta. As you know, we are precluded by international (interplanetary) agreement from interfering in the ongoing development of other worlds.

Most Sincerely

(signed) Octavius Bear

The letter never reached General Turmoil. The officers in charge of the facility at Exoplanet W who had escaped with their lives when the buildings and weapons took their precipitous plunges into the Red Dwarf star, had returned to Earth Alpha, Washington DC in a state of fierce revolt. They sought out the General and insisted he abandon his plans of cosmic conquest.

Needless to say, the General, still believing Moriarty was in a position of power refused to acknowledge or negotiate with the rebellious officers. Unaware that the Professor was marooned on a luckless exoplanet in the far reaches of the universe and believing the two of them could re-establish their insane plans, he ordered the rebels to stand down or be executed. A foolish move. Instead he was killed by them and died an agonizing death. His body was found floating in the Potomac. All plans for rearming and resuming efforts for cosmic conquest were summarily abandoned by the employees of The Business.

An official government investigation was initiated and The Business was shut down with all activities terminated, including interplanetary travel. When the cosmic conquest operations were revealed, senior officers were arrested. Staffs were disciplined. The General's demise was left unsolved. One villain dead and one irretrievably exiled for the rest of his life! Not enough! A cabal of ex-officers formed. They still had revenge in mind for Octavius Bear and his minions. He had destroyed their hopes and had left them professionally bereft. Several firebrands pledged retaliation.

Chapter Nineteen

The gentle heavenly breezes stirred the perfectly shaped celestial trees surrounding the mansion of Lady Juliet Armstrong, Baroness Crestwell (deceased). She and Pookie had returned from their adventures on Earths Alpha and Beta. She was chatting with Empress Sisi outside the Lipizzaner stables when Director Raymond appeared. "God's blessings on you two ladies and you too, Pookie. The threats are over. Well done, Baroness. Congratulations."

"I did very little, Raymond. Whatever credit there is should go to Octavius, his associates and Sherlock Holmes."

"Your modesty suits you well, Lady Juliet. Queen Mary and Magdalen would like to see you."

"Oh dear. I hope it's not another assignment."

"I think not but I shall not speak for them."

Once again they flitted to the magnificent glass tower at one end of the Elysian Fields - the Celestial Executive Complex. At the pinnacle sits the administrative headquarters of Her Majesty, Mary, Queen of Heaven. Director Raymond, Lady Juliet and Pookie flitted into the large golden anteroom where a group of angels were busily watching screens and directing activities.

The angel Orifiel was among them. He rose and bowed, flexing his magnificent wings in the process. "Lady Juliet, how good to see you again.

God's blessing on you and Pookie. I suppose you are pleased to be back in the heavenly climes."

"Oh, yes, Orifiel. That adventure was interesting but frustrating. We're glad to be in our celestial digs once again. Pookie is having a wonderful time playing with her chums in the Meadows and I'm just relaxing. I understand from Director Raymond here that the Queen wishes to see me."

"Yes, she does. Mary Magdlene is with her at the moment but I'll let her know you are here." He moved toward the cloud enclosed office door, knocked and on hearing a melodious voice say, "Enter" opened the portal and said, "Majesty, Lady Juliet and her dog are here as you requested."

"Oh, good. Send them in."

The Queen was as usual dressed in her simple robes and her serene face broke into a smile. Magda rose from her seat to embrace Juliet. "Well done, Baroness, well done!"

Mary agreed. "Yes, the cosmic threat has been averted thanks to you, Octavius Bear and Sherlock Holmes. Moriarty is alive but permanently isolated and while you and your cohorts had nothing to do with it, General Turmoil is dead and now secured in Hell."

Juliet shook her head. "I'm sorry we couldn't avoid his death but his own soldiers rose up against him."

"No, that was beyond your control. Are you ready for another assignment?"

Juliet winced. She had hoped this would be the last task for a long time. "Of course, my Queen. I am at your disposal."

Magda noticed the Baroness' expression and laughed. "Oh, Juliet, don't look so downcast. This will be quite a bit easier."

Mary looked at her. "Yes, you will shortly be called upon to lead a welcoming committee."

"A welcoming committee?"

"Yes, your new colleagues from Earth Alpha will be joining us soon. Octavius Bear, Bearoness Belinda and their very good friend, Mauritius Meerkat. This time they will be aware that they have entered Heaven. You must greet them and accompany them to their mansions among the Earth Alpha Celestial Community. Re-acquaint them with their families. Welcome them to the joy of God's Paradise."

"Oh, my. What a surprise! Will Holmes be with them?"

"No, Sherlock Holmes has a longer life to live. He still has many adventures to engage in even though he thinks he is retired. So has Doctor Watson and Mrs. Hudson."

Juliet looked down at Pookie who had been listening attentively and understanding that something important was about to happen. "Come, dear! We must go to the Pearly Gates with Raymond. Our friends will be waiting."

The Global News Report

World Mourns Loss of Beloved Celebrities

The fabulous multi-trillionaire Doctor Octavius Bear, his equally popular and wealthy consort, Bearoness Belinda Béarnaise Bruin Bear (nee Black) and their aide, Mauritius (Maury) Meerkat were killed last night when their private helicopter exploded near the Shetland Islands community of Lerwick. They were on their way to testify in the trial of Alaskan Senator Polonius Polar Black for the murder of his secretary. The Senator falsely claimed the Bearoness was his daughter.

Doctor Bear was famous for his sponsorship and expertise in a wide variety of sciences and technologies, his sole ownership of Universal Ursine Industries (UUI) and his worldwide reputation as a criminologist. Bearoness Belinda was the star aqueuse of the Aquabear Review - Some Like It Cold – and the owner/ director of Polar Paradise, a deluxe Shetlands resort. Mr. Meerkat was well known as a theatrical agent as well as the Great Bear's sidekick. A highly experienced pilot of fixed wing and rotary aircraft and owner of the last flying Concorde SST, the Bearoness was at the controls of the helicopter when it exploded.

The pair are survived by their twin teen-aged offspring, Arabella and McTavish Bear. They are also mourned by their team of companions, the so-called Octavians and their relatives and world-wide friends and associates. Funeral services will be conducted on a date yet to be decided at the Bear's Lair, the Cincinnati-based home of Doctor Bear and a memorial for them will also be held at the Bearoness' Shetlands resort – Polar Paradise. Since the Kodiak tycoon is American and the Bearoness has dual Anglo American citizenship both the FBI and Shetland Yard are investigating the explosion. Foul play by rivals is suspected.

Epilogue

(Earth Beta – Great Britain – Sussex Downs – East Dean- The Green –1905)

Several months after the untimely passing of Octavius, Belinda and Maury, raucous laughter echoed from Sherlock Holmes' cottage in Sussex where he was entertaining his crime fighting associates, alive and immortal. Mead and ambrosia were flowing and small snacks were being devoured alike by the mortal and saintly members of the group.

Among the still living, Holmes, Watson and Mrs. Hudson were in attendance.

In addition to her ethereal dog, Lady Juliet and Mr. Raymond made up some of the immortals, joined by the recently deceased Great Bear, Bearoness Belinda and Maury Meerkat. Guardian angels were in attendance.

Octavius was describing their reception in Heaven.

"We were graciously admitted to Heaven by Lady Juliet and the Director. He restored our memories of our previous visit and we met again with our parents and Maury's sister. We were welcomed by Queen Mary and Mary Magdalen who were most generous in their praise of our efforts to overcome the General and the Professor as well as our years of crime fighting."

"We have a spectacular mansion in the area of Paradise set aside for former Earth Alpha residents. Thanks to Mr. Raymond and Heavenly Real Estate! It's a combination of the Bear's Lair in Cincinnati and Polar

Paradise in the Shetlands complete with all the celestial accoutrements and a small ocean. Maury is with us, aren't you, pal! You must come and visit us, Lady Juliet. That goes for your little dog, too."

Pookie barked and wagged her tail. Maury ruffled the fur between her ears.

Maury added, "Absolutely. I got an early admission to heaven, I believe, courtesy of the Queen. Come see us! Please bring the Lipizzaner Horses, Pegasus and Hugh Unicorn. What a show they must make! Maybe I can help you put on a Saintly Spectacular."

Juliet laughed and nodded affirmatively.

Watson asked, "Have you discovered who blew you and your helicopter up and why?"

"No, we suspect the former minions of General Turmoil or possibly associates of the Senator intent on keeping us from testifying, but unlike a certain Baroness we know, we've agreed to enter Heaven without first solving the mystery."

Juliet blushed and laughed, looking at Raymond in the process.

Octavius chuckled, "Don't worry, Sherlock. We're not asking you to get involved. Frau Schuylkill, the Colonel, Otto, Giselle, Lord David, Howard, L.Condor and Chita are all working with Shetland Yard, the FBI, and your horse counterpart, Fetlock Holmes to figure this one out. So are the Ursulas and the staff of the Hexagon. We're assisting from Heaven."

Mrs. Hudson asked, "So your comrades - the Octavians - will persist?"

Octavius nodded, "That, of course, is up to them but I believe they have been too involved in crime fighting to give it all up. I'm sure they want to find who did the three of us in and destroyed a beautiful helicopter in the process."

Belinda agreed, "And the staffs of the Bear's Lair and Polar Paradise are carrying on. Our Twins are rapidly approaching maturity and will inherit our estates under an airtight testament drawn up by our lawyer, Wolford Wolverine. He, Frau Schuylkill and Colonel Where are the current executors. The resort and cruise line are busy as ever. UUI is prospering. The Hexagon is churning out its technological wonders. The Ursulas are even more capable than they were. Howard and Marlin are planning more cosmic ventures. And we have finally retired!"

She and the Great Bear both laughed.

Octavius looked at Holmes, "And what of you, Consulting Detective?"

"Oh, my bees and I are living the quiet, rustic life. I'm letting others take up the fight against criminals."

Watson, Mrs. Hudson and Juliet chuckled.

The Baroness raised her ethereal eyebrow. "I don't believe that for one second!

The End

ENDGAMES

Acknowledgements

These stories have evolved over a long period of time and under a wide range of influences and circumstances. I am indebted to many people for helping to bring my versions of Holmes, Watson, Mrs. Hudson, Lady Juliet and Pookie to the printed and electronic page. Thanks most especially to my wife, Virginia, for her insights and clever suggestions as well as her unfailing enthusiasm for the project and patience with its author.

To Steve, Sharon and Timi Emecz for their outstanding support of my twenty book Octavius Bear series, the four volume Glamorous Ghost collection and my other Holmes pastiches. To Derrick and Brian Belanger for publishing The Glamorous Ghost Book One and several of my other Holmes and Solar Pons efforts. To Dan Andriacco, Amy Thomas and David Chamberlain for their enthusiastic encouragement. And to all of my generous Kickstarter backers and reviewers.

To my sons, Mark and Andrew and their spouses, Cynthia and Lorraine, for helping to make these stories more readable and audience friendly. To Cathy Hartnett, cheerleader-extraordinaire for her eagerness to see these alternate worlds take form.

Thanks also to Wikipedia for providing facts and specifics of Victorian England and elsewhere. And additional kudos to Brian Belanger for his wonderful illustrations and covers.

Obviously, these stories are tongue in cheek fantasies and require the reader to totally suspend disbelief. I do hope they are entertaining fun. I'm not sure what Heaven is really like but I hope to find out one day.

If, in spite of all this support, some errors or inconsistencies have crept through, the buck stops here. Needless to say, all of the characters, situations, and narratives are fictional. Some locations, devices, historical figures and events are real.

About the Author

Harry DeMaio is a ***nom de plume*** of Harry B. DeMaio, successful author of several books on Information Security and Business Networks as well as the twenty-volume ***Casebooks of Octavius Bear.*** His four volume series, ***Sherlock Holmes and the Glamorous Ghost*** has been very well received. He is also a published author of pastiches for Belanger Books, the MX Sherlock Holmes and Dear Sherlock Holmes series. A retired business executive, former consultant, information security specialist, elected official, private pilot, thespian, disk jockey and graduate school adjunct professor, he whiles away his time traveling and writing preposterous books, articles and stories.

He has appeared on many radio and TV shows and is an accomplished, frequent public speaker.

Former New York City natives, he and his extremely patient and helpful wife, Virginia, live in Cincinnati (and several other parallel universes.) They have two sons, Mark, living in Scottsdale, Arizona and Andrew. in Cortlandt Manor, New York, both of whom are quite successful and quite normal, thus putting the lie to the theory that insanity is hereditary.

Comments are welcome. Positive or negative. His skin is thick. Of course, positive is better.

His e-mail is hdemaio@zoomtown.com

You can also find him on Facebook.

His website is www.tavighostbooks.com

His books are available on Amazon, Barnes and Noble, the Book Depository and other fine bookstores as well as directly from MX Publishing and Belanger Books.